AN UNEXPECTED LEGACY

BY MADISON GRANGER

An Unexpected Legacy

By Madison Granger

ISBN: 9798223186632

Dedication

To all who enjoy the worlds of paranormal romance.
May your alpha shifters be hot and sexy,
and your heroines be sassy, curvy, and kick-ass.

Acknowledgements

Without an editor and cover artist, my books would lack polish both between the pages and without.

Ravenborn Book Cover Designs and Personal Touch Editing add their own personal magic to my work.

An Unexpected Legacy was part of the Cocky Alpha Shifters anthology. I would like to thank Gina Kincade for allowing me to work with her, learning so much in the past year.

Chapter 1

Rafe Martin ran his hands lovingly over the surface of the long, polished oak table. Weathered by age and use, it was still a thing of beauty in his eyes. He'd spent long hours making it, taking pleasure in every aspect of the process.

Now he sat at the head of the table, a bowl of steaming stew in front of him. Smelling the delicious aroma all day, he was eagerly awaiting dinner. He closed his eyes in bliss after taking a huge bite. Dottie could create a fantastic meal from the most meager supplies, but the woman excelled at her stew. It was his favorite, and his aunt knew it.

He heard the commotion long before they approached his cabin. Shaking his head in resignation, he hurriedly got in a few more bites before the inevitable knock on the door. Passing a napkin over his mouth, he downed half of his sweet tea, then opened the door just as the man was going to knock.

"What is it, Riley?"

"Sorry to disturb your dinner, Alpha, but we thought you'd want to see this."

Rafe looked past him to see two others carefully carrying an injured man. They laid him down gingerly on his front porch. Rafe sniffed the air. He was wolf; whoever had done this meant business. The man was in no condition to shift.

"He's going to need a healer. Call Miriam." Turning to Riley, he asked, "Who is he, and where did you find him?"

"Found him in a ditch up the road. Best we could tell, he got dumped. Hasn't been able to talk much, pretty sure his jaw's busted in a couple of places, but he managed to get out a name."

"I'm not going to like the answer, am I?" Rafe studied the injured man.

"Afraid not." Riley took a deep breath. "It was Tom Sanders."

Rafe crouched down in front of the injured man and gently moved his head from side to side, noting the extensive bruising and swelling. The stranger moaned.

"It's all right, fella. You're safe, and we're going to see to your injuries."

An older woman, wearing jeans and a loose t-shirt, with snow-white hair hanging loose around her shoulders, approached the cabin.

"I hear you have someone for me to tend. What are we looking at?" Miriam Baxter, pack healer, winced at the sight of the injured man.

"We have a mess, Miriam. He's gonna need a ton of help."

"I'll say." Turning to the growing crowd milling around the porch, Miriam picked out two. "Danny, run to my cabin and get the stretcher I keep in the shed. Then you and Steve can carry this fella to my guest room. Handle him with care, boys. He's messed up pretty bad." Miriam affectionately patted Rafe on the arm. "I'll let you know how he's doing."

"Thanks, Miriam, appreciate it." Rafe ran a hand through his short hair, then scratched absently at his beard. "Riley, round up the enforcers and come back here. I'll call Kyle. We need to talk about this."

An hour later, Dottie was serving heaping slices of hot apple pie and mugs of coffee to a room full of wolf shifters. Rafe just rolled his eyes and kept his thoughts to himself. He thought Dottie was part magician because he damn well knew he didn't have any apple pie in his house that morning. Rafe waited until everyone had settled in, then he threw out the million-dollar question.

"Since it's probably going to be a while before we get any answers from our guest, does anyone know what's going on with Tom Sanders' pack?"

Riley and Mark glanced at Thane, who set his plate on the coffee table.

"We all know Tom has a problem with his temper, but the way I hear it, he's getting out of control. The fella Miriam is tending isn't the only one, but he's probably luckier than the rest because he got dumped in our laps."

"We gonna pay a visit, Rafe?" Riley asked.

"Since someone made it my business, we most certainly will, but not just yet," Rafe replied. "I want to talk to our guest to find out what happened to him and what's going on in that pack. I'm not walking into another alpha's territory unless I have the full story." He gave everyone a stern look. "That goes for all of you. No one goes off half-cocked looking for Sanders. Am I clear?"

There were no arguments, not that Rafe expected any. His men were all solid, loyal, and for the most part, level-headed. They were wolf shifters, though, there would always be a wild side to them.

"Riley, Mark, Thane, I want y'all to keep an extra close eye on the perimeters. I can deal with taking in one injured man, but I don't want this to become a regular habit or a dumping ground."

He turned to the big man sitting in the rocking chair. Quiet as usual, Kyle Martin waited for instructions. His brother had always been like that, quiet, unassuming, and as lethal as they came. The man was a gentle giant until it was time to go to work, which made him the best beta Rafe could have asked for. The man had his back 24/7. There was never any doubt about his loyalty and devotion to his older brother.

"Kyle, for now, keep an ear to the ground. Anything you hear about that pack and their alpha; I need to know."

"I'm on it." Kyle rose with surprising grace for a man his size. He nodded to the others and left as quietly as he'd come in.

Later that evening, Rafe was walking around the compound. Everyone was settling in, and things were peaceful. He liked this time of night, engaging with the sounds of the forest—crickets chirping, frogs croaking in the nearby creek, and the occasional hoots of an owl. Usually, he would let his wolf run, but it would have to wait this time.

Seeing Miriam's lights still on, he headed that way, wanting to check on the injured man. He wouldn't rush the poor guy for answers, but his curiosity was piqued. If the man had done something to deserve punishment, it would be a totally different story, although Rafe couldn't think of any crime deserving of such harsh disciplinary action. Then again, he was nothing like Tom Sanders.

Rafe's dominance and strength were well known among other packs. He demanded discipline and loyalty from his people, but he was fair, always listening to both sides of an issue before deciding judgment.

He knocked once but opened the door quickly when he heard screams from within. Sprinting to the guest bedroom, Rafe found Miriam's two sons, Danny and Steve, trying to hold the injured man down without inflicting further damage. Miriam was trying to soothe the man, but it obviously wasn't working.

"What's going on?" Rafe asked as he tried to make sense of the scene.

"Trying to set his broken bones is all," Miriam grunted. "He won't be able to shift until I can get him back together again, then have time to heal." She wiped her brow with her sleeve. "Poor guy isn't cooperating."

"Let me see if I can help." Rafe stood over the injured man, letting his alpha power wash over him. Rafe knew he wouldn't get the full effect because he wasn't a part of the Crossroads pack, but he'd recognize the power of an alpha. Sure enough, the man relaxed, falling limply in Danny and Steve's arms. They laid him down, and Miriam quickly went about her job. Thirty minutes later, it was done.

"Thanks, Rafe. That power roll helped," Miriam said with a sigh of relief. "I gave him a shifter dose of sedative so he can rest, hopefully, through the night. He should be able to shift by morning if all goes well."

"Let's hope so," Rafe agreed. "I'll come back then. Maybe we can find out who he is and what exactly happened to him."

Next morning, Rafe walked into his kitchen to find Kyle wading through a stack of pancakes. He arched a brow as he fixed himself a mug of coffee.

"Don't worry, there's plenty," Dottie assured him.

"You sure?" He sat down, eyeing his brother. "How soon will you have to make a grocery run?"

"Same as usual, every two weeks." Dottie slipped a plate in front of Rafe. "Let me know if you want more. I fried the bacon crispy, just the way you like it."

"Thanks, Dottie."

Kyle picked up a slice of bacon, made eye contact with Rafe, and bit into the crispy slice with relish.

"Enjoying yourself?"

Kyle nodded and helped himself to another slice of bacon.

Rafe pointed at the plateful of bacon with his coffee mug. "You *will* leave me some."

Kyle shrugged. "Of course, Alpha."

"Why are you here?"

"Dottie cooks for you."

"I thought that little omega was taking care of you. What was her name? Oh, yeah, Alicia. What happened to her?"

"Busy."

Rafe set his mug on the table and stared at his brother. "That crap works on everyone but me. Talk."

Kyle wiped his mouth with a napkin, pushed his plate away, and drank the last of his coffee. Rafe glared at him through the whole process.

"Talked to a guy who's in with a pack member of the Plantation Wolves. Seems their alpha has been helping himself to all the women in the pack, mated ones as well. He's passing around the omegas like party favors, and they're not handling the merchandise gently."

"Any idea what started all this? Tom's always been rough around the edges, but I don't think he's ever gone this far."

"Ever hear of a drug called Moonburst?"

Rafe thought about it before answering slowly, "I've heard the name, but I'm not familiar with it."

"Seems to be making the rounds with the younger shifters, and it's already a problem with a few packs, especially in the larger cities. Somebody's been playing with animal sedatives and cutting it with a human drug called fentanyl. It's a lethal mix. If you survive the dose, you get a high that makes you think you're invincible. It's also known to be an aphrodisiac, which is how most get started on it."

"Sanders got a hold of this stuff?"

"That's what I'm hearing. He's been sharing with his top boys, and they've been partying hard for a while now. How they're all still alive is a wonder."

"I don't get it, but it looks like I'm gonna have to deal with the trash." Rafe shook his head, sighing heavily. "Want to walk with me to Miriam's? I want to see if our guest is able to shift and can answer a few questions."

Kyle gestured toward the door. "Lead the way."

Chapter 2

Persistent buzzing penetrated Lyric's deep slumber, jarring her awake. She jolted upright, crying out in pain. Turning off the alarm, she fell back onto the bed with a groan and took a few deep breaths, trying to will herself to get up.

It wasn't as if she had a choice. She needed her job and couldn't afford to miss even one day. Her meager tips were barely enough to make her rent, utilities, and a few groceries every week. Her alpha made sure he got what he considered his fair share, which left her with nothing left over.

Trudging to the bathroom, Lyric turned on the shower, waiting for the water to heat. She had to time it just right because there wasn't a lot of hot water. Gathering her clothes, she dropped them on the corner of the vanity and slipped into the shower.

She hissed as the water hit her back. The lash marks would heal, but they were still fresh enough to hurt like a bitch. They would also scar, just like all the others. The alpha and his friends made sure she couldn't shift, guaranteeing the lashes would leave their mark. The last couple of months, he'd been extra brutal, taking out his anger on his play toys, as he called the single omegas in the pack.

As Lyric carefully dried off, over her shoulder, she caught her reflection in the full-length mirror tacked to the back of the door. She cringed at the sight of the raw, swollen stripes crisscrossing her back. The tip of the belt had caught her hips and rear, leaving red welts.

There was nothing she could do about it, and certainly no one she could go to or talk to about it. Sanders would see her dead first.

Dressing for work, she pulled her long, blonde hair into a high, tight ponytail. Glancing at the clock, she realized she'd dawdled long enough. It was time to dash out the door. She'd have to grab something at work for breakfast. Hopefully, Stan would have one of those breakfast wraps she loved so much, which were easy to eat on the run.

Pulling into the diner's small parking lot, Lyric hurried inside. She had just enough time to throw her purse into her locker and get her apron on before Nancy was yelling for her. The manager was a good person, but she liked to run a smooth operation, and in her eyes, which meant being early rather than on time. Lyric had cut it too close this morning.

"It's about time you graced us with your presence, Lyric." She looked down her nose at Lyric and harumphed her displeasure. "Table two needs to have their order taken, and table five wants more coffee."

"I've got it, Nancy." Lyric hurried to the front, coffee carafe in hand. Seeing to table five's needs, she scurried to the next table to get their order. And so it began, a normal day at the Blue Star Diner.

By the time her shift ended, Lyric was too tired to think of anything except going home and falling into bed. She wondered if she'd be that lucky. Rummaging in her purse, she pulled out the sandwich Stan had made for her.

He was one of the few people who seemed to care about her. Unfortunately, Stan was human and couldn't help. If he tried, he would suffer for it. Lyric knew and continually kept on a brave face, politely refusing his offers of aid, but she accepted the food. Barely making enough to buy decent food, she had no qualms about accepting his generous gifts.

Parking her rattletrap of a car, she limped to her house. Key in the lock, she turned the knob and heard his voice. She trembled, but there was nothing to do except turn around.

"Been waiting for you. What took so long?" Tom Sanders asked. He reached for her ponytail, winding it around his meaty hand.

"I just got off... I came straight home, I swear." Lyric's breath hitched, flinching at the contact.

"See that you do." He got in her face, his fetid breath making her gag. "Gonna need you tonight. Be at my place for seven." He jerked her head, exposing her throat. "Don't be late. The boys are looking forward to seeing you again." He leered as he licked the column of her neck.

"Ye... yes, Alpha. I won't be late." Her body shook, her gaze seeing only the ground.

He released her hair, throwing her against the door. "Get cleaned up. You smell like fried meat and grease."

Lyric's hand trembled as she opened the door. Dashing away the tears, she made a beeline for the bathroom. She'd clean herself so he and his 'boys' could dirty her again. Lyric stifled a sob. All the soap in the world couldn't scour away the dirt on her soul.

Once out of the shower, she sat cross-legged on the living room floor and looked around the tiny area with its rickety furniture and drab walls. What was here came with the place, and at the time, she'd been grateful to stumble up on it. Lyric didn't have the money to make it look any better. If not for her house, she'd be living in the compound with the other single omegas, and their lives were worse than hers.

Shifting into her wolf, she shook herself, whining at the soreness in her back and hindquarters. She hated subjecting her wolf to the pain but shifting was the only way to accelerate her healing. She had no illusions about the coming night. The Alpha and his gang would use her and the other omegas—they loved taking turns, eventually ending up in an orgy of horny males and helpless omegas.

It hadn't always been this bad. It used to be reserved for the full moon when the Alpha would dole out omegas to the unmated males. One night of degradation and she and the other girls could go back to their normal lives.

Since Sanders had discovered Moonburst, everything had changed. The drug's effect was fast and terrifying. The men became stronger and bolder, thinking they were invincible. The worst part was the drug was an aphrodisiac—their stamina increased five-fold, their erections lasting most of the night. They never climaxed, using the woman repeatedly. Then the fury set in. Not being able to release, they vented their anger on the women, beating, biting, and clawing. Lately, it had gone on night after night. Lyric prayed for death because she knew there was no other escape.

Shifting back, Lyric looked at the clock on the wall. It was almost time. Slipping her key into her pocket, she headed out the door. It was a short walk to the compound, where she would join the other omegas who'd been chosen for the night. Funny how she always seemed to be one of the chosen ones. She gave a mirthless laugh as she shuffled down the well-worn dirt path. Most people thought being chosen was an honor—if only they knew.

The girls mingled together, quiet and pensive, trying their best to go unnoticed. It wasn't meant to be, of course. The alpha's friends were never late to these parties. Being late meant running the chance of not getting the first pass of Moonburst. The booze and women were afterthoughts.

By now, Lyric could time when the drug would take effect. It was fast and hit shifters like a roaring freight train. She recognized the glazed look in their eyes, then the sniffing, as if they'd taken a hit of coke. Next were the crawls—Lyric didn't know what else to call it. The men would start rubbing and scratching themselves all over, as if something was crawling on them.

Then the rubbing went lower. They would fondle themselves until they were sporting obscenely huge erections. That's when the party began. Being a shifter, nudity never bothered any of them, even Lyric. It was part of who they were, but these men, under the influence of Moonburst, made everything lewd and disgusting.

They didn't make use of bedrooms; taking the women where they stood. Seven men and twelve to fifteen women, on any given night—on chairs, couches, and the floor—they seldom left the main room. It was crude and demeaning, but the women knew better than to say a word in protest.

"Lyric, get your bony little ass over here."

Gaze down, she shuffled over to the alpha. He had a grin wide enough to split his ugly face in half.

"Take care of Benny. His cock needs some lovin'."

With a ragged breath, Lyric fell to her knees. Before she could do anything, Sanders fisted her hair, snapping her head back.

"Make sure it's all tongue and no teeth. We wouldn't want to leave any marks, now would we?"

Their laughter drowned out the other sounds she heard in her dreams every night—men grunting and cursing, the women's cries, when they were hit for no reason or one of the men got too rough. This was their hell, and it would never end.

Chapter 3

Rafe woke to heavy knocking on the door. Grabbing his jeans, he pulled them up, zipping them halfway. Clambering down the stairs, he yelled, "Hang on, I'm coming." The knocking ceased, and Rafe growled low. "This better be good."

Miriam's youngest son, Danny, stood patiently waiting on the porch. When the door opened, he lowered his eyes submissively.

"Sorry to wake you, but Mom wanted you to know that guy shifted about an hour ago, and he's shifting back. She said now's the time to talk to him."

"Let me get dressed, and I'll be right over. Ask your mom to fix some coffee."

Danny grinned widely. "Sure will."

Grumbling under his breath, Rafe went back inside in search of a shirt and boots. Not ten minutes later, he was making his way to Miriam's. He texted Kyle to meet him there. Hopefully, they would at least find out the guy's name. Best-case scenario would be getting his story.

Rafe walked into Miriam's house to find a medium-sized gray wolf standing in the center of the room. His coat was coarse, flecked with brown. Spotting Rafe, he started trembling, his legs threatening to give out.

"Easy now." Rafe eased up to the wolf, crouching before him. "You don't have anything to be afraid of, even me. We're here to help you." The wolf chuffed, seeming to relax at his words. "Can you shift back?"

A short nod and the transformation started. Rafe moved back, sitting in an armchair to give the wolf room to shift. The process was slower than normal, probably due to his many injuries. It would be a few days before the man was completely healed.

Finally, a man lay on the area rug. Miriam handed him sweats and a t-shirt, which he took with a grateful smile.

"Thank you, Ms. Miriam." Dressing as quickly as possible, he sat on the couch. "Thank you, Alpha, for taking me in. They left me to die."

"Someone tossed you in a ditch on our lands," Rafe pointed out. "I wasn't going to leave you there." He studied the lean male. "Can you answer a few questions?"

"I'll do my best, Alpha."

"You can start by calling me Rafe. We're informal around here." His mouth twitched. "What's your name? I understand you're one of Sanders' pack, so I'd like to know what happened to you."

"I'm Eric Thompson. Until a few days ago, I was part of the Plantation pack." He swallowed hard.

"You need something to drink or eat?" Rafe needed to make the man comfortable if he was going to get anything out of him.

Eric's face reddened, but he swiveled to find Miriam. "If it's not too much trouble, can I have a bottle of water?"

"Of course, I'll be right back," Miriam said. "I'll fix you breakfast. You'll need to work on getting your strength back."

He flashed Miriam another grateful smile and turned his attention back to Rafe. "Sorry."

Rafe gave a dismissive wave. "Tell me what happened while Miriam gets your food."

"It's our alpha... Tom Sanders." Eric lowered his head, rubbing his temples. "He's always been a rigid man, but the past few months things have gotten worse." Eric let out a harsh breath. "About three months ago, two shifters showed up. They're not pack, but Sanders let them stay. It wasn't till later we found out they brought him some Moonburst to try." He looked up at Rafe. "You heard of it?"

Rafe's eyes narrowed as he inclined his head. "Recently."

"That's when things got rough. Sanders started having parties every night. It was always the same—his beta, enforcers, and the two suppliers. They started with the omegas. Those poor girls are going through hell. He used to give them to unmated males on full moons but now, it's every time he has parties. Sometimes..." Eric choked, unable to go on. Miriam passed him a bottle of water, and he took a few sips. He raised grief-stricken eyes to Rafe.

"Sometimes, the omegas aren't enough for them, and Sanders started calling in the mated females." His voice dropped to a pained whisper. "He showed up one night and dragged my mate out of the house." Tears streamed down his cheeks. "He passed her around to all the men. They raped her, hitting and choking her if she screamed. She came back home in the morning, bruised and bleeding." Eric let out an anguished moan. "My own mate wouldn't meet my eyes. She was ashamed." His hands trembled, the bottle of water falling to the floor. "She had no cause to be ashamed," he mumbled. Eric took a deep breath and raised his gaze to Rafe's. "My mate is pregnant with my pup. At least she was, and she's still there. Can you help me?"

Rafe leaned back in the chair, mouth drawn in a tight line as he went over everything he'd just heard. This was the kind of problem that could destroy the whole pack. It was more than an addicted alpha. It was Moonburst too, which was a bigger problem than Rafe could deal with alone. For now, he could handle

Sanders, but for the bigger problem—he would need help.

Rafe rolled his shoulders, then leaned forward. "I'll do what I can, but I need some detailed information. Can you do that for me?"

"Yes, Alpha." Eric's expression was a mixture of relief and gratitude. "I used to keep records for Sanders, pack numbers, and their information."

"That will come in handy. For now, I want you to focus on getting better. Do what Miriam tells you. You need to eat properly and shift often, so you can heal completely. Kyle and I are going to check into a few things." Rafe moved to leave, then turned back, "What's your mate's name, and is there a way to reach her?"

"Her name is Daphne." Eric took in a sharp breath. "I can give you her number."

"It'll probably be better if you call her, but don't do anything just yet. I might take a road trip to see exactly what's going on over there."

"Be careful. Sanders has men watching all the entrances to the camp."

"Good to know. We won't use those." He winked at Eric and left.

Rafe sat at the head of the table with Kyle at the other end, Riley, Mark, and Thane filling in the sides. He'd filled in his enforcers with everything Eric had shared earlier.

"So, how do you want to go about it?" Riley asked. "Want us to scout it out, see how things are set up?"

"I have an idea, but it will take a lot of finesse to pull off."

"Why am I getting the feeling we're not just gonna go in, stomp the alpha, and leave?" Kyle asked, his forehead creased with worry.

"I have a better idea." Rafe grinned.

An hour later, the enforcers left, shaking their heads. Rafe watched them leave, a smirk on his face.

"You really think we have a chance at pulling this off?"

Rafe shrugged, giving his brother a half-smile. "Won't know till we try, but to my way of thinking, it's the safest route for the females. We need to get them out of there safely—all of them. We can't just drive up and load them into an SUV, so we sneak them out in small groups."

"I don't know, Rafe. You have a lot riding on Eric's mate. We don't even know what kind of shape she's in right now. She might not get word to the other females, much less gather them together."

What his brother said was true enough. He was taking a huge chance, but it was the safest way to get the females out. If he tried to do it any other way, he took the risk of Sanders and his men hurting, possibly killing the females before he and his men could get to them. It was a long shot, but one he felt they could pull off. He just had to set it up right.

"We're going to find out right now about Thompson's mate because he's going to call her."

Returning to Miriam's cabin, Rafe found a calmer Eric Thompson watching television in the living room. According to Miriam, he'd eaten a big meal, gone wolf for a nap, and had just shifted back.

"Feeling better?" Rafe asked, scrutinizing the wiry shifter.

"Better than yesterday," Eric grinned. "Thank you, Alpha..."

Rafe waved him off once again. "I'm not one to let anyone suffer. On that note..." He pulled his cell phone from his back pocket, tossing it to Eric, who caught it one-handed. "Want to call your mate?"

Eric's eyes widened. "Yes," he replied, his voice raspy with emotion.

"Before you do, I want you to tell her a few things." Rafe sat next to him on the couch. Heads together, Rafe explained his plan to the shifter.

While Eric placed the call, Rafe went into the kitchen where Miriam was fixing a mug of coffee. She was smiling, but her eyes showed her worry as she handed him the cup.

"Do you really think this plan of yours is going to work?" Miriam searched his face for answers.

One thing about shifters, there were no secrets if they were in the same room. Their enhanced senses gave them an edge every time.

"Won't know till we try." He gestured to her to have a seat as he pulled out a chair, straddling it. "Let's see how this conversation goes." They sat together in silence as Eric called his mate.

Fifteen minutes later, Miriam and Rafe entered the room to find Eric hunched over, sobbing quietly. Rafe's phone lay on the low coffee table, wet streaks across the screen from the shifter's tears. Miriam sat next to Eric, draped an arm around his shoulder, and pulled him to her, hugging him tightly. Eric held the healer like a lifeline.

Rafe sat in the armchair and waited. He wasn't good at consoling people. He could break bad news as gently as possible, but he depended on others to be there for the ones in pain. He was sympathetic and compassionate, but he wasn't good with intimacy. Being unmated hadn't helped in that area, and Rafe wasn't looking for anyone to fill that spot.

Eric's sobs slowly subsided, his breath hitching. Miriam murmured in his ear, and he nodded, leaving the room to freshen up.

Miriam's pain-filled gaze met Rafe's eyes. "Daphne lost the baby."

"I figured that," he drew in a long breath. "It won't help the situation. Eric will be fighting mad or totally useless."

"I want in on whatever you have planned. I want Sanders to suffer," Eric said from the doorway. His fists were clenched tightly at his sides, and there was anger as well as misery in his red-rimmed eyes. "Because of him, I lost my child… our first. The healer told Daphne she might not be able to have another one."

Rafe looked at the man. "I want to ask you something." Eric stood silently in the archway, not quite meeting his gaze. "When this is over, do you want to remain with the Plantation wolves?"

Eric shook his head vehemently. "No way in hell do I want to stay there. I want to get my Daphne and get far away."

"Would you want to stay here at Crossroads?"

"That's a gracious offer, and I appreciate it, especially with all you're doing for my mate and me, but I just don't think I could stay in this area. I'll probably have to go lone wolf."

Rafe's eyes flashed, and Eric looked away. Going lone wolf was worse than going rogue. A rogue could survive, but a lone wolf wouldn't last long without a pack. Shifters were not meant to be alone; they needed the support and comfort of a pack. It was their safety net.

"Let me make a call for you. I have a cousin south of here, near Bellerieve. He leads a small pack. They're good folk. They run down in the swamps, and nobody messes with them. Does that sound like it could work for you?"

"Yeah," Eric's voice cracked. "That sounds real good."

"I'll call Ridge this evening and see if I can make that happen."

Chapter 4

The knock at the door was light, not like the pounding Lyric was used to when Sanders demanded entrance. She opened the door enough to peek outside.

"Lyric, I need to talk to you. It's important. Can you let me in? I don't want anyone to see me." A tiny brunette nervously looked over her shoulder as she spoke.

What in the world did Daphne Thompson want with her? She was one of the mated females, and they usually kept company with the other couples. The female was obviously nervous, her body language screaming it, even if she'd said nothing. Lyric had a feeling something else had happened, and it would be more bad news. Opening the door, she let Daphne in. The female scurried inside, then stood in the middle of Lyric's tiny living room.

"Have a seat." Lyric gestured to the couch. "It's not much,"—she shrugged—"but it's home. Can I get you some bottled water? It's all I have." Lyric cringed inwardly. Being an omega was bad enough, but Sanders had browbeaten her so badly, she couldn't help apologizing for every breath she took. She hated it but couldn't seem to stop.

"I'm fine, thanks." Daphne gave her a quick, nervous smile. She leaned back, crossed her legs, then suddenly sat forward, arms on her knees. "Look, I know we don't know each other well, but I'm here to help."

"Help with what?"

"I know what's happening to you and the others." She bit her bottom lip, nervously pulling at the hem of her shirt. "Sanders dragged me to one of his parties the other night, and it got rough." Her eyes misted, and she fought to hold the tears back. "I was pregnant. Eric and I were expecting our first pup. Anyway, I miscarried."

"Oh no, I'm so sorry." Lyric's eyes widened in horror. "Are you all right? Do you need me to call the healer?"

"She already checked me over. I'll have time to mourn later." Daphne dismissed her offer with a wave. "This is more important."

Lyric knew her confusion showed on her face, but she remained silent. Daphne's sense of urgency alarmed her, making her wait to hear the woman out.

"When I got home after Sanders' party, I was so ashamed—I didn't want Eric to see me like that. As you can imagine, he was furious with Sanders, and worried sick about me, but there was nothing either of us could do." Despite her tears, Daphne struggled to finish her story. "Anyway, after I promised Eric I would call the healer, he went to work like he usually does. Only he never came home. He didn't answer his phone, and when I called his boss, he told me Eric never showed up for work. That was three or four days ago." She covered her eyes with a hand. "I can't think straight, to be honest. He's been missing... until today."

"He came back?" Lyric asked.

"No, he called me about an hour ago," Daphne shook her head. "Sanders' men beat him so bad he couldn't shift, then they took him away, dumping him in a ditch on the side of the road."

"That's horrible!" Lyric cried, a hand to her throat. "Where is he?"

"He's safe. Some shifters from another pack took him in and healed him. Eric asked their alpha for help, and the man agreed."

"What kind of help?"

Daphne met Lyric's gaze, determination stamped on her grim face. "He's getting us out of here... all of us."

"What do you mean, all of us?"

"Exactly that. You, me, all the omegas. The alpha has offered sanctuary, if we don't want to stay with him, he said he'll find other packs to take us in. Eric and I are going down to Bellerieve to join the Bayou Crescent pack."

"I don't know, Daphne. If Sanders catches wind of this, he'll kill us. You know he will."

"That's why we have to do this fast. The Alpha wants to slip a few of us out every day. Three trips, we're all out. The full moon was last night. You know Sanders and his cronies will be too tired to fool with us for a couple of nights. It's the perfect time."

A tiny ember of hope flared in Lyric's soul. *Could they really do this? Was there a different... a better life for her and the others?*

"What if we're just going from one bad pack to another? What if this new Alpha is the same as Sanders? I'm scared, Daphne."

"I know, Lyric. I'm scared, too, but Eric swears this guy is the real deal. Says his pack are good people. They took care of him, not knowing who he was or what had happened." She scooted over to sit in front of Lyric, capturing her hands. "I have to get out of here. I can't go through that again. Sanders thinks Eric is dead, so I'm just another omega to him. I can't..."

"So, what are we supposed to do?" Lyric asked. She was terrified, but the thought of staying was worse.

"How many omegas are in the compound?"

Lyric tried to think, but her mind was racing in every direction. "Twelve, I think, at last count."

"Which four need to get out of there the worst?"

"Julie and Penny, they're both fifteen." Lyric didn't hesitate. "They won't last much longer with Sanders' bunch. Amanda and Valerie, they're older but weak. The others are a little stronger. They could probably hang on another night or two." She prayed she was making the right choices. It would be on her conscience forever if something happened to the others before they could get them out.

"Okay. Is there a way to contact them without actually going to the compound? The less activity on our part, the better. We don't want to make anyone suspicious."

"They all have cell phones, so I could text them, and if they want out, they can meet up here."

"They need to keep this to themselves, especially if they decide to stay, which could hurt us."

"They won't say anything. We're all terrified of Sanders."

"Tell them to pack only what they can't do without, then leave the compound separately and meet here at noon today. That's when Eric and the Alpha are coming for us."

Pulling her phone from her pocket, she started a group text. When she'd finished, she handed it to Daphne. "How's that?"

"It's the best we can do." Daphne forced a smile. "Let's hope this works."

Lyric looked around the tiny house one last time. Her small duffel bag wasn't full, which was a testament to how little she owned. Grabbing a framed picture of her parents, she hastily ran a finger over her mother's face, then stuffed it into the bag. Everything else, and there was woefully little, could stay behind.

If she was told to leave her car, she wouldn't bat an eye. It probably wouldn't make it to where they were going, anyway. Daphne had been closemouthed on the location, and Lyric couldn't blame her. They couldn't afford to have anything go wrong at this point.

A soft knock and a timid, "Lyric?" had her rushing to open the door. Julie stood at the door, clutching a backpack as if her life depended on it.

"Come in," Lyric said. "Did anyone see you?"

The frightened teenager shook her head. "No, I made sure. Penny is going to leave in ten minutes, so she should be here soon." She clutched at Lyric's arm. "Is it really true? Is someone going to help us get out of here?"

"It's true." Daphne came out of the kitchen, opening a bottle of water. "Eric said so, and he's never lied to me."

"I'm so nervous," Julie squeaked. "Noon can't get here fast enough."

"We're all feeling the same way," Lyric agreed.

Lyric pulled back the curtain a crack so she could peer outside. With a soft exhale, she opened the door to usher Penny inside. Julia rushed up, hugging Penny tightly. The girls sat on the couch, holding hands for comfort.

"Who else are we waiting for?" Daphne asked.

"Amanda and Valerie, but I don't know if Amanda is coming," Lyric answered. "When she texted me back, she said she had to think about it."

"She's really scared," Penny told them. "She's convinced Tom will find out."

"She won't say anything, will she?" Daphne turned wild eyes on Lyric.

"No, she's not like that. She's terrified of him, just like all of us," Penny reassured her. "She's too scared to do anything at all."

Lyric pulled the elastic from her hair, raking her fingers through the long tresses nervously. Her hands shook as she tried to put it back up.

"Here, let me get that for you," Daphne offered. With deft hands, she straightened Lyric's hair and pulled it back into a tight tail. "There, that should hold you." She patted Lyric's shoulders gently. "It's going to be all right. We just have to sit tight."

They waited nervously, watching the clock slowly tick the minutes. A knock at the door made them all jump. Julie let out a yelp, quickly slamming her hand over her mouth.

"I'm so sorry," she whispered.

Lyric tiptoed to the window, cautiously pulling the curtain back. She sagged with relief seeing Valerie at the door. Letting her in, Lyric tried to will the pounding in her chest to ease, but her nerves were teetering on the edge. She didn't know how much longer she could keep it together.

"Is Amanda coming?" Lyric asked Valerie. Once a vivacious redhead, abuse had taken its toll. Paler than usual, even her hair had faded, leaving her looking washed-out and way older than her true age.

"When I left, she still hadn't decided," Valerie replied sadly.

"Well, she has thirty minutes to make up her mind and get here." Daphne walked to the window, and pulled back the curtain, peeking out as Lyric had. "Lyric, do you have the girls lined up for tomorrow? Do they know to meet up here?"

Raking her fingers through her ponytail, Lyric looked up, startled. "Sorry, I was lost there for a minute. What?"

"The others," Daphne repeated. "Do they know what to do?"

"Yes, all four are ready to get out of here. I'm leaving my door unlocked. They're going to meet here, twenty minutes apart. They know to wait for Eric."

"Good enough," Daphne said. Shaking her hands nervously, she paced around the small room. "Just a few more minutes," she said, more to herself, than to anyone else.

As one, they all looked at the clock on the wall as it struck noon. Three pairs of haunted eyes fixed on Daphne.

"They'll be here. They'll be here," Daphne whispered.

The quick knock made them all jump.

"Daph? It's Eric."

Daphne flung the door open and hurled herself at her mate. He crushed her in his arms, carrying her back into the house. A mountain of a man with short dark hair and a trimmed beard followed him in. Looking over his shoulder, the big man checked the area, then quickly closed the door.

"Is everyone here?" Rafe asked.

Lyric stared up at the tall, muscular man. His gaze snapped to hers, and she immediately lowered her eyes.

"One... one woman didn't come, Alpha," Lyric stammered. She didn't have to be told or introduced to know he was the alpha. His presence dominated the room, making it seem even smaller. "She was too scared to try leaving."

"We can't wait any longer." Rafe rubbed his forehead with the heel of his hand. "We need to move now." He glanced at the women. "Gather your things and follow me."

The group cautiously followed Rafe outside, where a Suburban was parked in front of the house.

"Get in, quick," Rafe hissed, guiding them quietly to the vehicle.

When his hand touched Lyric's lower back, she jumped as if a charge had gone through her, but there was no time to wonder about it as she dove inside the SUV. As soon as she cleared the opening, Rafe shut the door and jumped in the passenger side.

"Roll!" he growled to the driver.

The Suburban took off, a dually pickup falling in behind them when they hit the highway. Lyric took a deep breath, scared to believe it had actually happened. After all this time, she was free of Tom Sanders. Looking ahead, she met the dark eyes of Rafe Martin. Her wolf whined, and she quickly lowered her eyes, showing submission to her new alpha. She prayed she wasn't leaving one bad situation for another.

Chapter 5

Rafe stepped out of the SUV, rolling his shoulders. The tension in the confined area had been almost suffocating. He'd tried to calm the women with his alpha power, but they weren't pack and beyond terrified. More than once, he wished he'd had the forethought to bring Miriam along. She would have known how to deal with the scared women.

Instead, he'd spent three hours in a Suburban listening to sniffles, crying, and whispers among the six huddled in the back. Kyle, in his usual stoic way, never said a word. It made for a long trip, and he had two more to look forward to.

Confronting Sanders would allow him to release the tension and pent-up anger he'd acquired since finding Eric literally on his doorstep. He had no qualms about ending Sanders and his boys. The more he heard of the other alpha's atrocities, the more he relished the coming encounter.

Miriam, Dottie, and a handful of other women met them at the truck, introducing themselves, and leading the females to where they would stay until things settled down. Rafe watched them walk toward the lodge. Usually, the building was for meetings or get-togethers. It was large enough to hold the entire pack, around one hundred, give or take a few. For now, it was being converted into a dormitory for the rescued women. Walking inside the large building, Rafe let out a low whistle.

Kyle sidled up next to him. "The females have been busy the last couple of days."

"I'll say," Rafe agreed. "Where'd we get all the beds?"

Bunk beds and twin beds lined both walls, leaving the center open. The women had set up two long tables and a dozen chairs for eating, and a couple of couches and armchairs to stand in for a sitting area. The lodge was equipped with a large kitchen in the back and two bathrooms, complete with showers. In no time, the building had been converted into a functional dormitory.

"We had a few in storage." Kyle scratched his head. "But I think some of the females donated the rest. I heard Dottie say a few pups outgrew their bunkbeds."

Rafe's gaze landed on the pretty blonde who'd spoken to him earlier. She was talking to Miriam, helping her get the others settled in. He wondered idly what she would look like with that long, golden hair down around her shoulders. Rafe shook his head. Where did that come from? He had enough on his plate. He didn't need to get distracted.

"Hey, Rafe, come give us a hand."

Riley and Mark were struggling with a couch that appeared a lot bigger than the door. Chuckling, he made his way over to the pair to see if he could help.

"I'm telling you, turn it this way and it'll slide right in," Mark insisted.

"It's not gonna fit." Riley snorted. "I don't care if you turn it completely around. It's too damn big."

Rafe backed up, eyeing the men struggling with the couch.

"Are you going to help or just stand there and watch us?" Riley asked.

"A smart man would check out his options to see what would work best," Rafe replied with a smirk.

"And which option would that be?" Mark huffed.

"You might want to unscrew those legs," Rafe chuckled. "That would give you about four more inches to play with. It should slide right in."

Mark and Riley set the couch down and stared at Rafe, looked at the legs of the couch, then the door.

Riley looked heavenward. "You don't think?"

Mark started laughing, "He *is* the Alpha." He unscrewed the legs on his end and gestured to Riley. "Come on, you know he's right. Take off the legs."

Grumbling, Riley unscrewed the legs, stuffing them in the bib of his overalls. Picking up the couch once again, they walked right through the doorway. "We'll never hear the end of this one."

"Nope, never gonna live this down." Mark was still laughing.

Rafe watched them set up the couch, the amusement still playing across his face. Turning, he leaned against the porch railing, enjoying the warmth of the sun. It wouldn't be too much longer before the days got shorter and the winds turned chilly.

"Alpha, may I speak?"

Rafe turned at the soft voice. Seeing the pretty blonde, he started. She wasn't pretty—she was drop-dead gorgeous. Her eyes were the color of cornflowers, the prettiest, clearest blue he'd ever seen. Full and pouty lips, with high cheekbones models would kill for.

"What's your name?" His voice came out rough and gravelly. She flinched, and he cleared his throat, trying again. "You don't need permission to speak to me. What's your name?"

"Lyric." She took a deep breath. "Lyric Taylor, Alpha."

"That's a pretty name, Lyric. I'm Rafe Martin, and you can call me Rafe. Is there something I can help you with?"

"No, I mean, I'm good." She nervously toyed with her ponytail. "I just wanted to thank you, for taking us all in, I mean. I... we really appreciate it."

Rafe massaged the back of his neck. She was as skittish as a colt. If he made the wrong move, she would take off. He sighed inwardly; she had every right to be nervous. Sanders had done a number on her, and the others. That wouldn't go away anytime soon, if at all.

"I'm glad I could help, and I want you to know, we're going to do our best to get the others out."

Lyric stared off into the distance. "What happens then?" she asked in a low voice.

"After the women are safe?" Her quick nod told him that's what she meant. "I'm going to take care of Sanders and his bunch. You'll never have to worry about them again."

"Thank you." Lyric let out a long breath. "You have no idea what a nightmare the past few months have been."

"No, I don't, but I've heard enough to know something has to be done. I'm not the type to let this kind of abuse slide."

She looked in his direction but didn't make eye contact. Rafe found himself wanting her to do that very thing. He wanted her to be comfortable around him, wanted to know what her smile was like when she met his gaze.

"You're not like him."

"No, I'm nothing like Tom Sanders. If you decide you want to stay here at Crossroads, you'll see the difference." He slowly eased toward her, not touching, but close enough. "Give it some time. I'd like you to stay."

"Thanks." Lyric smiled shyly at him, then took a couple steps back. "Guess I better go back inside and see what I can do to help."

"You do that. If you need anything, just ask. We'll do everything we can to make all of you comfortable."

Rafe rubbed his chin as he watched her curvy hips sway, graceful in her movements, as she walked back inside. His wolf whined when Lyric left. Since when did his wolf pay attention to who he talked to? She was beautiful, but she was an omega. His wolf shouldn't have even noticed her. It was more than a little odd, but he didn't have time to dwell on it. He had a running list of things that required his attention.

Thane and a couple of the other men were firing up the grills. Rafe headed toward the small picnic area, to see if everything was under control for the evening meal. Then he needed to get with Kyle and Riley about going after the next group of women. The next few days were going to be busy, and thoughts of a pretty, blue-eyed blonde were not helping.

Lyric rushed back to the safety of the women. Her heart thudded in her chest, heat flamed her cheeks, and even her wolf was riled up. She didn't understand her reaction to the alpha... to Rafe. The last thing she wanted was to be attracted to a man—any man—but the alpha? What was she thinking? There was absolutely no chance of that ever happening. She needed to put an end to that kind of thinking immediately. Her wolf whined, then bared her teeth. Lyric's hand went to her throat as she stilled, paying attention to her beast. She didn't understand and had no one to ask.

Lyric watched curiously as Eric and Daphne took two of the twin beds, tying them together. They moved it against the wall and began pushing the other beds away by a few feet. Realizing it would give them a sense of privacy, Lyric helped them rearrange the beds.

A handful of men showed up to talk to Eric, looked over the area, and left. A few minutes later, they came back with PVC piping and tools. Thirty minutes later, a frame had been erected around a ten-by-ten space, and sheets were rigged to hang from the frame. Just that quick, they'd prepared a private area for the mated couple.

"Can you help me put sheets on the beds?" Valerie handed Lyric an armful of linen then tilted her head toward the younger girls. "Miriam is having a private talk with Julie and Penny. She has a motherly vibe, and the girls are nervous wrecks." She gave Lyric a weak smile. "It's gonna take a while."

"It's going to take a while for all of us." Lyric knew how futile it was with everyone in the building having enhanced senses, but she lowered her voice. "I, for one, won't be able to breathe freely until Sanders is dealt with. I'll always be looking over my shoulder."

Valerie's eyes held nothing but sympathy. "Right there with you, honey." Valerie shook out one of the sheets, letting it settle across the bed. "So, who's coming tomorrow?"

"Susie, Carolyn, Amber, and Sarah," Lyric recited. "That's if nothing changes. The last trip will be for Ruthie, Dianne, Emily, and Vicky. I don't know about Amanda. I haven't heard from anyone yet."

"Do you think she'll come with one of the groups? They won't turn her down, will they?" Valerie looked over her shoulder, to see if anyone was paying attention to them.

"I don't think Rafe would turn anyone away."

"Rafe?" Valerie repeated. "When did you get on a first-name basis with the alpha?" She winked at Lyric.

"It's not like that," Lyric protested, heat flushing her cheeks. "He told me to call him by his first name." She squirmed under Valerie's scrutiny. "It's true. He said they're informal over here. It's not like back there." Lyric couldn't even call that place home. The word stuck in her throat.

She'd never been happy there, even as a child when her parents were alive. Tom Sanders was the type who wasn't happy unless everyone was miserable, and he'd succeeded in that respect. Plantation pack was the worst of the worst.

By the time they got the beds set up and each woman had claimed their spot, the sun was lowering. Dottie and Miriam insisted they join the others outside for their evening meal.

"I promise you won't be swamped by the entire pack. It will only be those you've already met and their mates. We want you all to feel comfortable, and promise not to rush any of you," Dottie assured them.

That was how Lyric ended up at a picnic table laden with trays of barbeque chicken, ribs, and sausage. Dottie and Miriam disappeared into one of the log homes, reappearing a few minutes later with bowls of potato salad and beans. Loaves of still-warm French bread were set on the table along with dishes supplied by other women of the pack.

"I don't think I've ever seen this much food," Lyric whispered to Valerie.

"Me, either." Valerie's eyes were wide as she watched dish after dish appear on the picnic tables.

"Ladies, help yourself," Rafe said as he circled the table. "Plates and utensils are at the end. There are drinks in the coolers." He bent closer to Lyric and Valerie, careful not to crowd them. "There's plenty of food, so don't be shy. No one goes hungry around here."

Lyric watched as Rafe moved on, chatting with everyone as he made the rounds, eventually getting a plate and loading it with food.

"Is he for real?" Valerie asked.

"I'm not sure, but he sure seems like it," Lyric murmured.

"Dottie told me if we didn't want to stay here, the Alpha would find other packs to take us in," Valerie said as she looked around. "If this place is for real, I'm not leaving. The people are nice, and the compound is neat and well-tended. Who wouldn't want to stay here?"

Lyric tended to agree with her. Not that she had much to compare, but this was Utopia next to what she'd known. Julie and Penny walked up, laden with platters of food.

"Can we sit with y'all?"

"Of course, you can." Lyric gave a wide smile and pushed over, making room for the girls. As the girls settled in, she asked, "Are you two okay?"

"A lot better now," Julie said, around a mouthful of potato salad.

"Miss Miriam talked to us," Penny added. "She said we could go to her anytime we got scared or nervous about stuff."

"Lyric?"

"Yes, Julie?"

"Things really are going to be better now, right?"

Lyric caught Rafe looking their way. He smiled at her, then went back to his conversation.

"Yeah, honey, I really think it's going to be a lot better."

Chapter 6

"Make sure the boys are ready to go in the next few minutes. We need to make this as smooth as possible... in and out." Rafe patted Kyle on the shoulder and turned around to find Lyric walking up to him.

"Morning, Rafe."

"Good morning, Lyric," he responded, watching her closely. She seemed different this morning, not as skittish as yesterday.

"I want to go with you to get the other women."

"I'm sorry, I can't allow that." Nope, not skittish, more like, determined.

"Why not?" Hands on hips, she looked up at him, not quite making eye contact.

"I can't take the chance on anything happening to you. I don't want you getting hurt," Rafe explained.

"I can take care of myself."

Rafe just looked at her.

"I won't get in the way." Lyric swallowed hard. "But you need me. Those women don't know you and the other men. They won't go with you."

She was making a valid point, one he'd thought about long and hard, but what she was asking of him was too much. He didn't want her going back there for any reason. His wolf was totally on board with his decision.

"You have their numbers, Lyric. Text them and let them know what the plan is."

"You're going to need me there," she insisted.

Rafe let out a long, slow breath. "Don't fight me on this, Lyric."

She stepped back, her hand against her throat. Rafe felt like swearing up a blue streak, but the last thing he wanted was to scare her. She had to know he was doing this to protect her.

"Lyric, text them now." For a second, he thought she was going to argue with him. Instead, she pulled out her phone, her fingers flying across the small keyboard. She bit her bottom lip, probably trying to hold back the tears swimming in her eyes.

Rafe felt like a total jerk, but he couldn't take the chance. If Sanders came around—if he hurt her... he couldn't get that far. All he saw was red, and his wolf was growling, which was never a good sign.

Lyric handed the phone to him, her chin jutting out a bit, and Rafe huffed. He knew he wouldn't like this. Looking at her phone, he found she'd sent the text as a group message. Five women hysterically messaging Lyric, most of them refusing to leave with strange men.

Kyle looked over his shoulder. "Better today than tomorrow."

Rafe rolled his eyes.

"What's tomorrow?" Lyric demanded.

Kyle stared at Lyric, then at Rafe, obviously waiting for Rafe to take her down a peg. No one talked to him like that, not even his own blood family.

"This one time..." Rafe shook his head. "Kyle, let it go."

Lyric's head bobbed back and forth between Rafe and Kyle.

"Never talk to me in that tone again, Lyric," Rafe said in a low voice. "I can't allow it, do you understand?"

She lowered her head. "I'm sorry, Alpha."

He captured her hands, closing all space between them. "Look at me, meet my eyes." She slowly raised her gaze to his. "I won't hurt you or punish you. That's not my way, but I am Alpha, and I demand respect. Do you understand?"

She nodded, tears trickling down her cheek. "I'm sorry."

"Accepted. You and my brother both have valid points. It's better to let you go with us today, though I'm still against it. We need to get those women out of there."

"But tomorrow?" She asked softly.

"After we get the women out, I'm staying behind to deal with Sanders."

"But you can't ... not by yourself... he has others..." Lyric's voice rose with each word. Her gaze pierced Rafe, and his wolf whined, not wanting her upset.

"I have others, too, and they will be with me, but this is my fight. I'll be all right, but I want you and the other women here safe. I won't be disobeyed on this matter. Do you understand?"

"I do, Rafe." She shook her head vehemently. "I didn't mean to cause you any strife, but I need to help."

Still holding her hands, Rafe felt a flow of calm wash over him. He looked at Lyric curiously but said nothing. Stepping back, he let out a breath, the tension easing between his shoulders.

"Let's load and get moving." He turned to Lyric. "Get in and text those women. I want them at your place and ready when we get there."

Closing the back door after Lyric got in, he slid into the passenger seat. Kyle slid him a curious look. He leaned against the head rest, closed his eyes, and murmured, "Not now, Kyle."

He knew his brother wanted to know what was going on between him and the new omega, but it was a question he couldn't answer. There was something, but damn if he could figure it out.

His wolf got excited every time they got near her, and not for the first time, he wondered about it. It shouldn't happen. He didn't understand why it was happening. He wouldn't lie to himself, he was attracted to the woman, but was holding a tight rein on those feelings. She'd been through too much. Lyric probably couldn't stand the touch of a man... yet she let him hold her hands a few minutes ago and hadn't pulled away.

He scrubbed his face, scratching his short beard. He didn't have time for this, and his wolf just sat there looking at him expectantly. For the love of... *Mate*— what the hell?

Lyric texted everyone, and they'd all calmed down, promising to be ready. Even Amanda had been talked into going with them. Lyric was glad to hear it. She wouldn't last much longer if she stayed. Of course, none of them would at the rate the men were going through them. Moonburst was turning them into monsters.

A part of her wished the drug would kill them all, then felt terrible for even thinking such a thing. Six months ago, such an awful thought would have never entered her mind. She blamed Tom Sanders for so many things but making her become someone she wasn't proud of was the worst. She had to believe things would get better with the Crossroads pack. She needed to believe Rafe Martin would protect them.

Just like that, her thoughts were on the dark-haired, handsome Alpha. Even chastising her, he'd been gentle but firm. She'd never known anyone like him. Her wolf was certainly interested, and there didn't seem to be any talking her out of it. She pranced around with her tail in the air every time he was near. Lyric was just a lowly omega; she didn't have a chance in hell of someone like Rafe Martin noticing her... no matter how bad her wolf wanted it to happen.

Getting up her nerve, she leaned closer to Rafe, and asked, "When this is over, what happens then?"

"What do you mean?" Rafe unbuckled his safety belt and turned to face her.

"I mean to us. What comes next?"

"Well, I guess first thing is y'all decide where you want to stay. You are all more than welcome at Crossroads, but if some aren't comfortable here, I can help find them another pack. Then, we help you adjust to life at Crossroads. Everyone in the pack works, and there's no shortage of jobs in town. We can arrange transportation to get you where you need to go. It's going to take time, Lyric, but we're here to help all of you build a new life."

She thought about what he said, trying to process it.

"Is something else bothering you?" Rafe asked.

"No, I guess I'm just trying to take it all in." She smiled at him. "I don't expect you to understand, but what you're offering is more than any of us ever dreamed of." She looked down, then met his gaze full on. "Thank you, Rafe." Leaning back against the seat, she stared out the window, preparing for a new life.

"Lyric, wake up, baby." Rafe's low voice woke her up. "We're almost there."

She smiled as she roused. Did he just call her *baby*? Almost there? Her eyes widened as she sat upright, staring out the window, seeing familiar landmarks. They were close. She grabbed her phone and checked for messages. She'd missed a few. Typing furiously, she filled the women in on their location.

"They're all there, waiting," Lyric told Rafe.

"Good. We're going to make this quick. You go in and get them back here as fast as possible. You remember how we did it yesterday?"

"I'm ready."

The SUV pulled up in front of Lyric's home. She sprinted out the vehicle and hurried to the front door.

"It's me, Lyric," she whispered, as she knocked. The door flew open, and five women crowded around her. "Let's go. Get in the Suburban. Keep quiet. We'll talk later."

As Lyric helped the last one in, she heard someone yelling at her. Turning, she froze. It was Roy, Sanders' beta.

"Hey! Where you think you're going?"

Rafe pushed her into the truck, slamming the door behind her.

"Roll, we've been spotted!" Rafe growled. Kyle peeled out as Rafe put a cell phone to his ear. "Riley, we're gonna have company. Be ready." He ended the call and turned to Lyric, reaching for her hand. "Lyric, look at me. Are you okay?"

Gasping for air, she turned wide, terrified eyes to Rafe. "The others, Rafe, what about the others?"

"We're gonna get them, baby, I promise. Give me a minute, okay?"

She nodded, turning to the women beside her. They all turned anxious gazes on her.

"Rafe's gonna fix it. He's got this."

"Lyric, what are the names of the other four women and where are they?"

"Ruthie, Dianne, Emily, and Vicky," she responded immediately. "They're at the compound."

"Listen closely," Rafe instructed. "Call them now and have them get to your house asap. They're coming with us today."

"Trucks coming," Kyle announced.

"Kyle, pull over. I'm getting out. Get the women home."

"The hell you say," Kyle bit back. "Lyric, you know how to drive this tank?"

"Yeah, I can drive it."

"You know the way back to Crossroads?"

"Yeah."

"Kyle…" Rafe growled, the sound filling the Suburban.

"I'm not leaving you, man. Don't even think it. Lyric is solid. She has this."

Kyle met Lyric's gaze in the rearview mirror, giving her a wink.

"I can do it, Rafe," Lyric assured him. "Just be careful." Her wolf had gone into a full-blown panic mode, and she knew exactly how the beast felt.

Kyle pulled over sharply, skidding to a stop. "C'mon, Lyric."

She bounced out and back into the driver's seat without taking a breath.

"Move, baby girl, don't look back," Rafe growled, as he pulled off his shirt.

Lyric peeled out, shooting gravel and rocks from the side of the road. As she sped down the highway, she looked back once to see Rafe and Kyle bound down the road as two of the largest wolves she'd ever seen.

Chapter 7

Showtime. Rafe felt power surge through him as his wolf ran back to face Sanders' men. He doubted seriously the alpha would be with the first wave of attack. The man was too cowardly. He'd send everyone else first to take him out. Rafe growled. Try again, dickhead.

With curses ringing in their ears, Rafe and Kyle ran past the truck containing Sanders' men, running hard to the pack's land. Rafe wouldn't fight on the highway where innocent humans could come up on them. No, he was taking this back to their turf. Ducking through the trees, he and Kyle made for a clearing. Rafe knew

Riley, Mark, and Thane would be right behind them. They would level the playing field, one way or the other.

Rafe ran to the far end of the clearing, turned around, and waited. He didn't have long to wait. Two large, dark brown wolves, growling ominously, stalked onto the grounds, crunching leaves and twigs beneath their huge paws. Rafe bristled with pent-up rage. He was so ready for this, but they were going to have to come to him. He was patient that way.

The wolf on the right sprang toward Rafe. Recognizing him as Sanders' beta, Rafe met him in the air. Both wolves went for the other's throat, back claws raking underbellies. They fell to the ground with a loud thud, snarling and snapping, neither one letting go. Rafe sprang back and lunged again. He locked onto Roy's throat, shaking him as if he was nothing more than a rag doll. Roy whined, his back legs clawing furiously for purchase.

Tearing himself loose from Rafe's grip, the beta lunged low for Rafe's legs. He got in a lucky swipe, tearing through the muscle on Rafe's flank. The coppery smell of blood filled his nostrils, as he fell in a pain-filled heap, struggling to right himself before Roy attacked again.

The other wolf circled around to Rafe's other side, but Kyle flew at him, taking the wolf down in a heap. Teeth and claws claimed their damage as they rolled in the dirt, locked in their own battle.

Roy circled Rafe, trying to find an opening on his injured side. Rafe stood tall, despite heavy bleeding, fangs dripping as he snarled his rage. When Roy leapt, Rafe was ready for him. Rafe ducked, going for Roy's soft underside. Jaws locked on a rear leg, crushing the bone with an audible snap. The wolf yelped, falling to the ground. Rafe swiped him to his side with a large paw and snapped down on his throat, ripping through muscle, sinew, and bone. The wolf lay still at Rafe's feet.

Kyle had dispatched the other wolf, circling the lifeless body to stand at Rafe's side. Together, they waited for Sanders to make his appearance. It was only a matter of time. Rafe hoped Lyric had gotten in touch with the other women and they were all safe, waiting to be picked up. No sooner had the thought crossed his mind than Sanders staggered up to them, holding a young woman in front of him, a knife to her throat.

"You thought you were gonna come in here and steal my females, Martin? What gives you the right? Go get your own whores."

Rafe shifted seamlessly, standing nude in the middle of the clearing. The inside of his thigh was far from healed, but he would never show weakness, especially to an opponent. He eyed Sanders and the woman. She turned fear-filled eyes toward him. He hoped she wouldn't do anything stupid. One slip of the knife, and she was gone.

"That's the Moonburst talking, Sanders." Anger crashed through Rafe. "You've abused these women for the last time. They want out, want a safe place, far away from you and your boys."

"That so? We'll see about that." Nostrils flaring, his lips drew back in a snarl as he slid the knife across the female's throat, blood welling along the blade. Throwing her and the knife to the ground, Sanders shifted. The shift to wolf was unsteady, taking more time than usual.

Rafe closed his eyes in grief. There was nothing he could have done to save the woman. The drug was controlling Sanders and his wolf, hindering his shift. Even under the circumstances, Rafe couldn't bring himself to take advantage of an opponent before a completed shift. Rafe waited. Three wolves lurked behind Sanders, but they didn't concern him. His enforcers would have his back.

Shifting back, he waited. His flank injury would hinder, but not incapacitate him. This wasn't his first fight or injury. Sanders growled and advanced, his eyes gleaming a brighter-than-normal hue. Too late, Rafe realized his folly. Still under the influence of Moonburst changed not only Sanders' behavior but his wolf's as well. Movement and judgment would be erratic, making his wolf unpredictable, which could be lethal for Rafe.

Getting his feet under him, Sanders ran at Rafe, hurling his body with the force of a battering ram, and the impact sent Rafe flying backward. Before he recovered, Sanders was on him, furiously snapping and biting, trying to get a deeper grasp on a vulnerable area.

It took everything Rafe had to keep Sanders away from his throat. His leg, weakened by the first fight, was useless to push against the other wolf. With only one good hind leg, he was desperately trying to keep his balance.

The fight seemed to go on forever, neither wolf gaining a distinct advantage. Rafe could hear the other wolves barking and growling but thankfully, no one interfered. Suddenly, like a switch had been turned off, Sanders faltered, stumbling on a turn. Rafe wondered if the Moonburst high was wearing off.

Rafe didn't hesitate, going straight for the throat and not letting up until he heard the satisfying snap of the wolf's neck. It was over—he'd defeated the Alpha of the Plantation pack. Howling his victory, his wolves joined him, the sound echoing for miles.

Shifting, Rafe stood slowly, scanning the area. Tom Sanders, his beta, and three enforcers lay dead on the ground, along with one of the women. He walked over to her body, and lifeless eyes stared up at him. Such a senseless loss. It was going to hurt to tell Lyric. His wolf whined, and Rafe sighed. She meant something to his wolf, and damned if she wasn't beginning to mean something to him.

The wind gusted, mixing the scent of dead leaves and dirt with sweat and blood. Kyle approached him slowly, as did Riley and Mark.

"Where's Thane?"

"He went to get the females."

"Mark, why don't you meet up with him? Take the dually and get them home. Riley, Kyle, and I will tend to this mess." With a nod, Mark sprinted down the dirt road toward Lyric's old house.

"What do you want to do with the bodies?" Riley asked.

"Think he's got a backhoe around here?" Rafe scratched at his beard. "I'm all for dumping those five in a hole and setting a torch to them." He hitched a thumb at the woman. "She's going to get a proper burial."

Riley nodded. "Lemme see what I can find."

"I'll go with you. We're gonna need a couple of shovels and a truck to get home," Kyle added.

Rafe was left alone, surrounded by death—a tragedy that should have never happened to a pack of shifters. Picking up the dead woman, he walked to the back of the property, heading for a copse. There, he would lay her to rest. In the worst way possible, she'd found peace.

Rafe winced as he slid out of the truck. It was going to take another shift before that slice healed completely. Roy had struck deep, severing muscle and tendon.

People poured out of their homes when the truck slid to a stop in front of his cabin. He was tired, dirty, and bloody, but he knew he had to deal with this first. His people needed to know he was all right and what had happened. It was his duty to protect his pack and to keep them aware of what was going on.

He climbed the two steps to his porch without showing pain. Leaning against his railing, he faced the sea of faces. His gaze sought Lyric, and spotting her on the fringe of the group, he felt calmer.

"It's over," Rafe stated. "Sanders and his men are dead. Unfortunately, we lost one of the females we went to rescue. She was given a proper burial at the back of the property under a stand of trees."

"I defeated Plantation's alpha, which makes me their alpha. I won't split myself between the two packs, nor do I plan to integrate the two. I'll be going back to see how many shifters are there and if anyone is capable of leading them. My decision will be based on what I find."

"For now, I want everyone to welcome the Plantation women who chose to come here. They are now a part of Crossroads until they decide otherwise. Help them settle in and embrace them as part of our pack."

Rafe backed from the railing, turning to go inside his cabin. Everyone eventually went back to their homes. From his link to the pack, Rafe knew everyone was satisfied that all would be well. No one was alarmed or agitated.

Sorrow shredded his insides as he walked inside his cabin. Because of a drug, lives had been lost. While

Sanders had never been an ideal alpha, he'd still held his pack together. Now, the responsibility fell on Rafe's shoulders. He would deal with the problem, but it would wait. For now, he wanted a shower, and a shift. Tomorrow was another day.

Several hours later, Rafe heard a light knocking on his door. In wolf form, he scented the air. Lyric. He yipped happily. Rafe shifted, reaching for sweats on a nearby chair. Pulling on a t-shirt, he went to the door. He opened it slowly, and Lyric's scent filled his nostrils. Heat coursed through his veins, desire flickering to life.

"I wanted to make sure you were all right... see if you needed anything," Lyric said hesitantly.

He opened the door, gesturing for her to come in. When she walked past him, he inhaled deeply, filling his nostrils with her scent. She was sunshine and wild roses, everything fresh and vital. His wolf yipped, wagging his tail, wanting to get closer—*Mate*—Rafe shook his head, trying to clear his senses. It couldn't be... she couldn't—there was no way, but his wolf seemed so sure, so accepting.

"I wanted to thank you for taking care of Ruthie." She hurried on, seeing the confusion on Rafe's face. "The woman you buried."

"I didn't know her name," he said in a low voice, rubbing the back of his neck. "The others... are they all right?"

"Yes, for the most part." She seemed to come to a decision and closed the distance between them. "They need to settle in and come to terms with everything that's happened." She rested her small hand on his arm. "They'll be fine, but—I'm worried about you."

Calmness seeped into Rafe, filling him with a sense of security and well-being. He looked down at Lyric, trying to figure out what happened every time he was around her. Lyric's cornflower-blue eyes looked up at him serenely, her full, pouty lips barely parted. The urge to kiss her was overwhelming, and he didn't know if he had the will to deny himself—or his wolf.

Saying nothing, he cupped the back of her head, bringing her closer as he lowered his mouth to hers, kissing her tenderly. Her breath warmed him as he angled her mouth for a deeper kiss. Her softness melded against his hard planes, fitting perfectly, as they got lost in the kiss.

After forever, he dropped butterfly kisses on her cheeks, pulling back slowly. His wolf chuffed happily, the word *Mate* branded on his brain. He still didn't understand it, but his wolf was sure he wanted Lyric. To him it was a done deal. He wanted to claim their mate.

Chapter 8

Lyric walked back to the temporary dormitory without stumbling. More than a little dazed, she held two fingers to her lips, still reeling from his kiss.

He'd never said a word, just kissed her. Lyric had never been kissed like that. She'd never known tenderness. In one heart-wrenching kiss, Rafe had given her that and so much more.

Lyric's wolf was ecstatic, letting her know in no uncertain terms he was their mate. She, on the other hand, couldn't accept it quite that readily. He was alpha, she was omega, and—the two didn't go together—at any time.

Did Lyric find him attractive? Hell, yes. She'd have to be dead not to be attracted to him. He personified everything tall, dark, and handsome. Dark-brown eyes of liquid chocolate—she could get lost in them for days. His hair was a rich dark mahogany, shot with highlights of caramel. Her fingers itched to run through the thickness to see if it was as lush as it looked. His beard, neatly trimmed, enhanced his strong facial features. He was chiseled from granite, over six feet tall, every muscle cut in deep relief—strong, broad shoulders, his abs a work of art, tapered waist, narrow hips, and the Goddess paid full attention to that tight, round rear, not neglecting powerfully muscled thighs and calves. The man was perfection.

Lyric, on the other hand, was... no one who should entertain thoughts of Rafe Martin in such a way. Her wolf snarled, baring her teeth, which brought her up short. Her beast didn't agree with her assessment. Climbing the short steps, she remained on the dormitory's narrow porch, leaning against the support beam.

Appeasing her wolf, she assured the beast she was by no means unattractive, but Lyric was average—height, weight, everything. She guessed her best features were her long, blonde hair and blue eyes. At least, she'd been complimented on them a few times by the other women of the pack, but looking in a mirror, Lyric never saw anything special.

"Lyric, is something wrong?"

She looked over her shoulder, seeing Daphne standing in the doorway.

"Nothing's wrong. Are you all right? Do you need some help with something?"

"You always worry about everyone else. When do you take time for yourself?" Daphne eased forward, wrapping an arm around Lyric's waist.

Lyric shrugged, looking at the neat picnic area surrounded by large, shady trees. The pack's land was much like the people she'd met—full of life, healthy, and vital. She thought about the Plantation pack with their crowded, dingy homes and dirt roads, and the comparison was ludicrous.

"I can't change who I am or my situation," she told Daphne. "If I'm helping others, I don't dwell on me."

"But you have that chance now," Daphne exclaimed. "You're already in a better situation—don't think I'm the only one who's noticed the way the Alpha watches you."

"What do you mean?" Lyric shot her a panicked look.

"Lyric, he watches every move you make. Everyone's noticed. There's talk of Rafe finally taking a mate."

"A mate! Well, that's certainly not going to be me." Lyric fought hard to calm her wolf. The beast wanted Rafe for her mate and would settle for nothing less. "Alphas don't take omegas for mates. They need someone strong, to help lead the pack." She turned sorrowful eyes on Daphne. "That doesn't begin to describe me."

Daphne was deep in thought before she finally responded. "I think it's more between our wolves than our pack rank. If his wolf wants to claim you, it's pretty much a done deal." She eyed her knowingly. "What does your wolf tell you? I would be shocked if she's been quiet all this time."

"She's noticed him," Lyric admitted. "Please don't tell anyone," she pleaded anxiously. "I'm not sure what to make of everything. My wolf thinks Rafe is her mate and hasn't let up since he rescued me."

"Oh, honey." Daphne hugged Lyric tightly. "You can't fight Fated Mates." She stepped back, searching Lyric's eyes. "Why would you want to?"

"It's not that," Lyric tried to put her jumbled thoughts together, trying to figure out how *she* felt, not her wolf. "Rafe is incredible. It's me... I'm not good enough."

"Don't you ever let those words pass your lips ever again." Daphne glared at her. "You are every bit as good as any woman here and better than most." Daphne planted her hands on her hips, pinning Lyric with a hard stare. "If anyone needs anything, they go to you. If the younger girls need advice or even makeup tips, they go to you. If anyone is going through a hard time, you're the first one offering help. Lyric, you're the most caring person I have ever met, and I have no doubt Rafe Martin has already noticed it."

Lyric's eyes welled with unshed tears. Daphne's words had touched her deeply. She honestly hadn't realized others felt that way about her. Rafe had certainly noticed her. That kiss was unforgettable.

"Speaking of the devil, guess who's headed this way?" Daphne murmured. She gave Lyric a pat on the shoulder. "Think I'll go inside. Eric is probably wondering what happened to me."

Lyric side-eyed Daphne. With their mate bond, Eric knew Daphne was perfectly safe. Watching as Rafe neared closer, she swallowed hard.

"You *are* good enough," Daphne hissed before going inside. "Remember that."

Approaching the porch, Rafe looked up at her. "Can I talk to you?"

Lyric nodded.

"Let's go over there where we can sit." He gestured toward the picnic area, reaching for her hand as she walked down the steps.

They could sit and have privacy to talk.

Rafe pointed to a glider swing, never letting go of Lyric's hand.

"I need to apologize for what happened back at my cabin."

Lyric lowered her head, fighting back tears.

"I'm not apologizing for kissing you." He lifted her face with a finger. "I'm apologizing for the way I did it. You must think I'm a Neanderthal. You've been through too much already. You didn't deserve that."

Lyric stared into his dark liquid eyes, too stunned to say anything. Rafe sat forward, elbows propped on muscular thighs, and ran a hand through his hair. Lyric wished it were her fingers doing that. His hair looked so thick and soft.

"You know as well as I do, when our animals tell us something, we need to listen. They're better attuned to things around us, and they're never wrong." He glanced at Lyric. She was watching him, but her head was lowered. She twisted her fingers nervously in her lap, waiting for the worst.

Turning to face her, he said softly, "Lyric, look at me." When she did, he captured her shaky hands, rubbing them until her breathing eased and she calmed down.

"My wolf noticed you immediately." He chuckled low, the sound warm and mellow to Lyric's ears. "He wasn't the only one."

Her eyes widened, not sure what he was telling her.

"I've been drawn to you from the first, but you need time to settle and heal. My wolf isn't as patient as I am. He says you're our mate."

Lyric's jaw dropped, and she hurried to close her mouth, embarrassed by her reaction. "But I'm just an omega."

"True," Rafe agreed. "But not *just* an omega. I happen to think you're a very special one."

"What do you mean?" Lyric was getting more confused by the minute.

"I've been doing a little research."

Lyric looked at him strangely. When had he found time in the past two days for research?

"I don't sleep much," he confessed with a light laugh. "Anyway, every once in a rare while, an omega is born with special qualities. These omegas are nurturers and healers, and once they're claimed by an alpha, they possess the ability to calm the pack, keeping them grounded and spiritually peaceful."

"I don't have those qualities," she protested.

"But you do." He clasped her hands tightly in his. "I just have to see you, and a sense of calm enters me. I've watched you with the others... always helping." Rafe gently traced a finger along her cheek. "Those omegas make the best mates for alphas. My wolf knew it immediately. I just had to figure it out for myself."

"But..."

"No buts." Rafe kissed her lightly. "You're my mate, Lyric, but I'm not pushing you. We'll get to know each other, and you need to heal. When the time is right, we'll know." Rafe stood, tugging her hand gently. "Let's get you back to the lodge. You need to get some rest."

His arm draped around her shoulder, he walked her to the door, then kissed her tenderly.

"Sleep well, my omega."

Chapter 9

Rafe sat in the creaky swivel chair, with his elbows on a battered desk, massaging his temples with a thumb and index finger.

"Shifters don't get headaches," Kyle remarked.

Rafe turned his head toward his brother, his hand never leaving his temples but exposing his middle finger.

"You try to figure out this mess and see what happens," he retorted. "This pack is so screwed up. No one knows what's going on. They were all too terrified of being pulled into Sanders' Moonburst club."

"Is there even a pack left?" Kyle moved a dingy curtain aside to look out a filthy window. "From the looks of it, everyone is leaving."

"Most of them are." Rafe shut his eyes for a moment. "Some are heading to the West coast; others have distant family in Texas." He stood, stretching. "I'm trying to keep a list of who's staying. Hopefully, one of them is an alpha or a strong enough beta to take over."

"Any prospects?"

"A few, two alphas and three betas. I'm waiting on their decision. They're discussing it with their families."

"Understandable," Kyle answered as he rifled through filing cabinet drawers.

"You know it's hard to have a real conversation with you." Rafe's mouth twitched.

Kyle looked up. "Your point?"

Rafe rolled his eyes.

"It's all good, bro." Kyle grinned. "Besides, look what I found." He pulled out a manila folder, handing it to Rafe. "This must be the records Thompson was talking about. It's a list of pack members."

"Last entry is three weeks ago." Rafe scanned the sheet. "This will help a lot. I'll get Lyric to go over it with me."

Kyle's brow raised. "What's going on with you and her, anyway?"

Rafe's first instinct was to say nothing, but that would deny his feelings—and betray Lyric.

"She's my mate," he said quietly.

"For real?"

"Straight up," Rafe admitted.

"You claimed her yet?"

"No, I'm not rushing her. We talked about it, and we're going to wait, let her get over Sanders and his mess.

"Makes sense."

"Let's get out of here. We can't do anymore today," Rafe said as he headed toward the door.

"We're gonna stay here?" Kyle asked, his face showing his disgust.

"Nope," Rafe stated quickly. "I can rough it with the best of them, but this place is just nasty. We'll get a motel room in town."

"Thank you," Kyle said with a sigh of relief. "I'm so grateful I'll even pay for the room."

Rafe feigned shock. "I'm holding you to that."

Pulling the ringing cell phone from her back pocket, Lyric stared at the unknown number. She bit her bottom lip in indecision—answer it or ignore it. Taking a deep breath, she answered it, a quaver in her voice.

"Hello?"

"Lyric? It's Rafe."

Her whole body went limp with relief that it wasn't anyone from the old pack. She was still having trouble believing that nightmare was over. Looking for a private spot to talk, she stepped outside.

"How can I help you, Alpha?"

"Lyric," the soft warning growl came clearly over the line.

"I'm sorry... Rafe."

"That's better. First, how are you holding up? Is there anything you need?"

"I'm fine, really." She couldn't believe he was taking time out of his day to check on her. No one had ever worried about her like this. "Miriam and Dottie have everything in hand. We have all we need. Thank you."

"Good, that's what I like to hear," Rafe said. "If you're not busy, I'd like your help."

"Of course, what can I do for you?" He needed *her* help?

"Kyle found a list of Plantation pack members. We're pretty sure it's the one Eric was keeping. I wanted to go over it and a list of names of the ones who left today and the one's planning to leave. I need your help to make sure if it's worth keeping the pack together. I've got a few who could be potential alphas, but I want your feedback first."

"I'll do the best I can." Lyric was stunned. This was no little thing he was asking. Her opinion would impact the future of an entire pack. She was both thrilled and humbled he had asked for her opinion. He could have gone to Eric, instead, he had called *her*. Her wolf stared at her, giving her a knowing look. *Mate.* Lyric rolled her eyes.

It didn't take long to go over Rafe's list. With her knowledge of the members, she had a fair idea who would help the pack and who would be better moving on. Plantation pack had never been large, and the number was considerably smaller now, but it was still worth salvaging if someone stepped up as alpha and beta.

"Thanks, Lyric. I'll have to stay here another couple of days to set things in motion, but after that, Plantation should be able to function as a pack again."

"Rafe, thank you." Lyric sniffed. "Thank you for taking care of the pack and everything. At least now, they have a standing chance of making it."

He hesitated before answering, and Lyric wondered if she'd said something wrong.

"Do you want to go back?" His voice was low and hesitant.

"To Plantation? No, I never want to see that place again," she answered firmly.

"Good. I'd let you go if it was what you wanted, but I wouldn't be happy about it."

Lyric could hear the relief in his voice, and she felt a rush of tenderness.

"I like it here at Crossroads." She took a breath and let him know how she felt, at least a little. "I think I can be happy here."

"My little omega, I'm going to make sure you're happy. I'll see you soon."

Lyric held the phone to her ear long after Rafe had ended the call. Tears swam in her eyes as it hit her full force—Rafe Martin really cared about her.

Rafe couldn't help smiling as he ended the call with Lyric. He felt a wave of calm just talking to her, but his feelings for the blonde omega went further than that. He accepted his wolf's claim that Lyric was their mate, but he was also having feelings for her as a woman.

Lyric was different from any female he'd met. She was grounded, and her natural nurturing instincts spread to everyone she met. She would be a valuable asset to the pack, but again, it was more than that. He wanted Lyric by his side, wanted to know her better. He enjoyed talking to her, and they worked well together. Rafe could see himself making a life with her by his side as his mate. He could easily envision a future with her. He'd never felt that way about any other woman. He wasn't lying when he told her he'd make her happy. He planned on making it a daily goal.

Rafe woke rested and eager to get back to the Plantation pack. He wanted to wrap things up on this end so he could get back to Crossroads—and Lyric. Her image stayed in his mind, and his wolf was getting restless. It was time to get things moving. Luckily, his brother seemed to be more than eager to get back too.

"I picked up some breakfast we can eat on the way if that works for you," Kyle offered, holding up two large bags from a local fast-food place.

"As long as you got coffee along with it."

"In the truck." Kyle gave a toothy grin. "You might want to hurry before it gets cold."

Rafe looked around the room. "I'm ready. Let's head out."

Leaving the motel, Rafe inhaled deeply. The air was cool, crisp, and invigorating. Autumn was setting in fast. It wouldn't last long though. Louisiana wasn't big on the third season, usually going straight from summer to winter. With all the evergreens, there wasn't a big color change with the leaves.

Regardless, he preferred the cooler temperatures. He felt more energetic, and his wolf readily agreed. He was overdue for a run. Rafe would take care of that as soon as he returned home. He wondered if he could get Lyric to accompany him. His wolf was in full agreement, his tongue lolling out.

They pulled up to the house Sanders used as an office to find two men waiting for them. Rafe recognized them as ones he'd spoken to earlier, Sam Lawson and Billy Harris.

"Morning, gentlemen," Rafe greeted them. "What can I do for you?" He'd talked to them about taking over the pack and was hopeful they'd reached a decision in the pack's favor.

Sam stepped forward, Billy right behind him. "We've decided to stay. Billy said he'd stay if I took over as alpha and agreed to be my beta."

Rafe's mouth curved into a smile as he stuck out a hand. "That's the best news I could've hoped for." Shaking Sam's hand, he added, "Let's go inside and make this happen."

An hour later, Rafe stepped into the bright sunshine and punched the air. It was done. Plantation pack had an alpha and a beta. The pack would get together this evening for a Peaceful Transference of Leadership, and Rafe would be free to return to Crossroads. His spirits soared—he could return to Lyric.

Rafe and Kyle spent the rest of the afternoon preparing for the meeting and small ceremony. It wouldn't take long but there were still things to tend to. Crossroads wasn't a wealthy pack, but they were all hard workers, and together, they had made a community they could be proud of. Plantation hadn't had that opportunity under Sanders' rule, and it showed in the rundown homes and dirt roads. It would take time to rebuild their pack and community.

Rafe went over the structure system with Sam while Billy shadowed Kyle, picking up pointers and tips. People slowly started milling around the common area. Nervousness and doubt were tangible emotions, and Rafe kept rolling power waves over the group, trying to instill ease.

More than once, he wished Lyric was with him, but from what he'd learned, her power wouldn't envelop the pack until they were mated.

Rafe looked out over the crowd of faces, looking back at him expectantly, glimmers of hope on their worn faces. He turned to Sam.

"Ready to do this?"

Sam nodded, his eyes glowing amber, his wolf right under the skin.

"Plantation pack, come forth!" Rafe let his wolf surface, his own eyes glowing brightly. Everyone crowded together to witness the change of power. "I am Rafe Martin. I am your Alpha." Rafe's voice carried to the last shifter, clear and concise. "This pack has known pain, suffering, and poverty. As of now, all that is in the past. Under the Law of Shifters, I am calling on a Peaceful Transference of Leadership."

"As of today, Sam Lawson and Billy Harris will become your Alpha and Beta. They will set things straight within Plantation pack and take you on a new road, one of substance and merit. You will be bound to them as you are to me."

Sam stepped to Rafe's side. Facing each other, they clasped forearms.

"From this day forward," Rafe intoned, his voice gravelly with power, eyes glowing bright amber. "Sam Lawson will lead Plantation pack as alpha." Waves of power spiraled around the two men, then blasted out among the crowd. The small pack knelt, baring their necks to the new alpha.

Power diffused as it settled into each shifter. From now on, each pack member would acknowledge Sam as their alpha. Rafe was free of his obligation. The crowd dispersed, only to set up tables and produce a feast for the pack.

"You're not going to stay for the celebratory meal?" Sam asked.

"Thanks, but I need to head back to Crossroads." Rafe shook his head.

"Got a hot date?" Sam joked.

"You have no idea." Kyle winked.

"All right, you two," Rafe growled but tempered it with a rueful smile. "It seems one of your women is my mate, and I'd like to see her."

"Really?" Sam's eyes brightened. "Which one?"

"Lyric." At that moment, Rafe realized he was proud to tell others he had a mate and who she was.

"Well, congratulations! She's an exceptional female. I'm glad to hear she's going to be your mate. She deserves some good in her life." Sam clasped his hand, shaking it vigorously. "I wish the two of you all the best."

"Thanks, appreciate it," Rafe replied. "If you need anything, be sure and call. I'll be happy to help."

Once in the truck headed home, Rafe let his thoughts drift to a beautiful blue-eyed blonde.

Chapter 10

The sounds of hushed whispers woke Lyric. She laid still, trying not to move about as she tried to locate the source. Daphne and Eric had a makeshift curtain canopied around them, affording them privacy from prying eyes, but it did nothing to buffer the sounds of the couple's lovemaking.

Lyric wiped away a tear. What she listened to wasn't anything like her experience with Sanders and his men. What she heard was tender and loving. She dared to wonder if it would be like that with Rafe. Would he be a gentle lover? Would he take his time, knowing what she'd been through? Her heart told her yes, and her wolf had no fear of the handsome alpha.

A part of her wanted to accept him as her mate and start a new life, but the bigger part of her was terrified. She wasn't afraid of Rafe, she was afraid of herself. She didn't know if she would be able to give of herself. She needed to get past the fear but wasn't sure she would ever be able to... not completely. Maybe that's what Rafe meant when he told her he would give her time to heal.

Daphne and Eric finally settled into a sated sleep, leaving Lyric with her thoughts of a tall, dark, and very handsome alpha. Determined to take one day at a time, she drifted off into an uneasy sleep.

A ray of sunlight played across Lyric's face, waking her from a deep sleep. Covering her eyes with an arm, she heard movement and excited whispers from Daphne and Eric's corner. Propping up on an elbow, she tried to see what was going on. A suitcase, duffel bag, and boxes sat on the floor by their bed. Daphne and Eric were talking quietly, then Eric left the dorm.

"What's going on?" Lyric asked as she slipped out of bed.

"We're going to Bellerieve today," Daphne answered excitedly. "Zane Landry is coming to get us. We're going to stop by our old place and get the rest of our things, then head to Bayou Crescent."

"Today?" Lyric felt a sense of loss. In the last few days, she'd grown close to Daphne and was going to miss the female shifter.

"I'll stay in touch, I promise," Daphne said, coming over to hug Lyric.

She hugged Daphne back, but knew the words were empty. Once she joined the new pack, Daphne would be busy with her new life. Shifters preferred to stay in their packs, and they didn't venture out unless it was necessary.

"Is anyone else going with you?" Lyric asked.

"Yes," Daphne said hesitantly. "Amanda and Amber are going too."

Lyric nodded as she processed the information. Amanda would probably thrive with a smaller pack. She was a timid woman who needed constant reassurance. Amber, on the other hand, was confident and eager. She was just trying to find a good fit.

"I'm sure they'll be happy with the Bayou Crescent wolves. Rafe speaks highly of the brothers."

"Eric spoke to Rafe about the Landry brothers. He said Ridge was a fair Alpha, just not to be put off by him because he was on the quiet side."

"I'm sure that won't be a big issue," Lyric teased.

"Sounds like a total opposite of what we had at Plantation," Daphne agreed. "The change will be nice."

Lyric helped Daphne pack their few items, then went in search of Amanda and Amber to say her goodbyes.

Excited murmurs caught Lyric's attention as she walked outside the dormitory. She looked up to see Kyle dropping Rafe off, then pulling his truck off to the side of the cabin as another SUV pulled up behind them.

The two brothers greeted the driver with handshakes and backslaps. Lyric had a feeling this was Zane Landry from the Bayou Crescent wolves. Sure enough, the three headed her way. Lyric ducked inside the dorm to let the others know their ride was here.

It took a few minutes for introductions to be made, and belongings to be situated. Zane Landry was a handsome man, tall and tanned. His piercing blue eyes contrasted sharply against his raven-black hair. Lyric didn't miss the interest in Amber's eyes as she shook hands with the good-looking shifter. Maybe there would be more than one mate-bond between Plantation and the new packs.

As Lyric said goodbye to her packmates, she could feel Rafe's heated gaze on her, and it was taking everything she had to keep her senses about her. Finally, Zane loaded his new charges, and they headed down to Bellerieve and their new lives.

Standing on the dorm's porch, she watched Rafe speaking to a couple of people. Turning, he spotted her and stood still, watching her stare at him. As if invisible cords were set free, he strode toward her, and she met him halfway.

Rafe framed her face with his large hands and kissed her deeply. He didn't seem to care they were out in the open, in front of his pack. Lyric fisted his shirt, returning the kiss. She wouldn't let it bother her, either. When he ever-so-slowly ended the kiss, he trailed a gentle finger down her cheek.

"I missed you, little one."

She gave him a shy smile. "I missed you, too."

He bent down to her ear, whispering, "I need to freshen up. Will you come to my cabin in an hour? I want to spend some time with you." He searched her face. "Just talk, I promise. Nothing more."

"I... I'll be there," she stammered. Lyric watched him walk away, her heart hammering in her chest. A small part of her wished for more, but he was right. They needed to start slow, and she was grateful for his patience. Heading back inside, she decided to make good use of that hour and freshen up herself.

Valerie, Julie, and Penny fussed over her, insisting on at least fixing her hair. Never one to wear a lot of make-up, she only wore eyeliner and mascara with a touch of gloss. The teens brushed her hair until it shone like spun gold. Working their magic with curling irons, her hair draped around her shoulders in soft waves and curls. Lyric blinked, staring at her reflection in the mirror. She couldn't remember ever fixing her hair or even wearing it down, for that matter.

"Thank you, ladies," Lyric said. "I really appreciate all the effort you put into this. I don't look like myself."

Valerie shushed her. "Girl, we didn't do anything. Your hair is already gorgeous. The girls just played with it. You're always pulling it back in a ponytail, so no one knew you had a gorgeous head of hair."

"We just want you to look nice for the alpha," Julie said as she hugged her.

"It's time," Penny told her. "You don't want to be late."

"Yeah, that fifty feet from here to there might take a while," Valerie joked.

Hoping she wouldn't appear too eager, Lyric walked over to Rafe's cabin exactly on time. Knocking lightly on the door, she heard him crossing the room. He opened the door, a welcoming smile on his face, and Lyric melted a bit. For the first time, she saw him as a man, not the alpha. He looked relaxed, happy, and was drop-dead gorgeous when he really smiled.

"Come in. I'm setting the table now. We can eat in just a minute."

"Eat?" She knew her confusion showed on her face.

"My bad." He grinned as he guided her to the kitchen with a hand on the small of her back. "I forgot to mention that part. I called Dottie earlier and asked her to fix something for us." He stopped, gazing down at her. "You haven't already eaten?"

"Umm, no," she replied hesitantly. "I wasn't really hungry earlier."

"Good." He beamed at her. "Dottie makes the best lasagna. All I have to do is pop the dinner rolls in. Come, sit and talk with me." He snapped his fingers. "Wine... would you like a glass?"

"Yes, that would be nice." Watching Rafe in the kitchen, she realized he was as nervous as her. She couldn't figure out why, but there it was. She hid her smile behind a hand. It was really rather sweet. As he bustled around the kitchen, she glanced at his home. It was truly a spacious cabin. The kitchen was large with all modern conveniences and plenty of workspace. She sat at a table that easily sat twelve, and it didn't crowd the kitchen.

A wide archway led to the living room. Exposed beams gave the rustic room the illusion of even more space. A leather couch and two large, overstuffed armchairs were arranged comfortably around a low, square coffee table. A fireplace centered the back wall, and a large screen television was mounted on another wall. She wondered what the rest of the house looked like. It had to be as nice as what she saw here. Her thoughts wandered to Rafe's bedroom, and she pulled that thought to a screeching halt.

Rafe placed a glass of wine in front of her, then pulled out a chair. He sipped his own wine, then covered her free hand with his own.

"Are you settling in all right? Do you or any of the others need anything?"

"I'm fine… we're all good, Rafe. Stop worrying so much. You rescued us from a living hell. Staying here is a piece of heaven."

"I guess I won't stop worrying until I get all of you situated in your own places." He gave her a rueful smile. "We have a few empty cabins on the property, but not one for all of you."

"I'm sure we can work around it." He was really worried about their situation and Lyric strived to find the right words to ease his stress. "The girls all bunked together at the old place. I was the only one who had my own house."

"You could stay here." Rafe's eyes flashed amber, then quickly went back to their usual brown. "I have a guestroom you could use."

"I'm not sure..." Lyric faltered.

"I know... I'm sorry," Rafe hurried to apologize. "I'm rushing things. I didn't mean to."

"It's okay." She patted his large hand. "Let's figure out something for the others first. How about that?"

The timer went off, and Rafe winked at her. "Let me get the rolls out of the oven, then we can talk about it over dinner. How does that sound?"

"Sounds good." Lyric sat back and took a sip of wine, enjoying the tart freshness. "Is there anything I can do to help?"

"Nah, I've got it." Slipping the rolls into a small cloth-covered basket, he set them on the table, along with a fresh green salad and the lasagna. "Is there anything else you need?"

Lyric looked over the table. "Goodness, no. This is perfect." She smiled to herself at the blatant relief crossing his face.

He served her, then watched as she took a bite, making sure she liked it. Lyric was touched yet disconcerted. She was so unused to the attention, not that she wasn't enjoying every moment. She just needed to accept it.

Discussing the available cabins, Lyric discovered they were all two-bedroom and fully furnished. Rafe produced a notebook and pen, and by the end of the meal, Lyric had assigned all the girls to cabins. The teens, Julie and Penny would have to share a room, but everyone else had their own space. Of course, that left her.

Rafe looked over her list. "You didn't put yourself on here." He pulled at the collar of his shirt. "Do you want to stay here with me?"

"Would that be an imposition?" Heat rushed to her face. She was putting herself out there, something she didn't normally do.

"I would like nothing more." He reached for her hand, stroking it gently. "You're my mate, Lyric. I want you close to me." Relief suffused his features. "My word is good, though. I'm not rushing you. You'll have a room of your own."

Lyric placed a finger against his lips. "I trust you."

He kissed her finger, then took her hand in his. His dark eyes met hers, staring right into her soul.

"You will never regret it."

Chapter 11

Rafe surveyed the room, making sure everything was in order. The last few days had been busy, but the dust was settling, and he was making sense of everything once again.

It hadn't taken long to get the women settled in the cabins. They all seemed extremely pleased with the arrangements and he hadn't heard a complaint from any of them. Dottie and Miriam were taking the women into town to apply for jobs. They'd work out transportation as the need arose.

Rafe and his wolf were extremely happy with Lyric moving in. As agreed, she settled into the guest bedroom. She had insisted on going with the other women to search for a job, even though Rafe assured her it wasn't necessary.

He didn't care for the idea of his mate working for a living, but he hadn't claimed her yet and knew it meant a lot to her. She needed the independence holding down a job would give her. It was part of her healing process, and he wouldn't begrudge her that.

Today, he would be busy with other issues. Calling on the alphas of the largest packs in Louisiana, he asked for a meeting to discuss the rampant spread of Moonburst and what they could do to curtail, if not eradicate, the drug. Not surprisingly, all were in agreement and promised to clear their schedules at the first available date. Rafe hadn't wasted time in planning the meeting, and all were due to show up at any moment. Each alpha would bring his beta and an enforcer, if so inclined. His own enforcers had the grills going, preparing food for the shifters. The rest of the pack would pitch in and help, as they always did.

Even though Ridge Landry didn't head up one of the largest packs, Rafe had included him in the list. Rafe figured since he'd taken on a few of Plantations' people, he had a right to know what was going on. Speaking to him the night before, Ridge had agreed, letting him know Zane and their younger brother, Cole, would be with him.

"They're coming in," Kyle reported as he walked into the lodge. "Ridge and his brothers are here, and so are Sam and Billy."

"Good, I'd like to speak to them first before the others get here," Rafe replied.

"I'll let them know and keep an eye out for the others," Kyle said as he went back outside, hailing the men.

Within minutes, Sam Lawson and Billy Harris entered the lodge. Shaking hands with Rafe and exchanging pleasantries, they took seats at the long table. The door opened again to three tall, well-built men looking around as they entered. Ridge Landry, the eldest and Alpha of Bayou Crescent wolves, wore his dark hair slightly longer than current trends. His hazel eyes narrowed, missing nothing. Zane, middle brother and beta, sported raven-black hair and piercing blue eyes, whereas Cole, the youngest and pack enforcer, had dark auburn hair and green eyes. They had the same parents, so genetics apparently had a field day when the brothers were born.

Rafe was not only related but friends with the brothers and glad to see them again, even if the situation wasn't under the best circumstances. He quickly filled them in on what he had in mind.

"I'm calling in the major alphas today." He addressed the Landry brothers as he gestured toward Sam and Billy. "Moonburst almost destroyed the Plantation pack. I was lucky to have Sam and Billy take over. Leading two packs isn't my cup of tea, and I don't have enough room here to merge them.

"I'm hoping if we present a united front, we can each venture out to smaller packs and sniff out any who are dabbling with the drug. I honestly don't know how widespread this stuff is, but we need to keep it away from our packs." Rafe lifted his head as he heard Kyle speaking to someone right outside the room. "Guess the others are here."

As Rafe rose, the door opened, and Kyle escorted the men inside. He made quick introductions to the ones already there. Alpha of the New Orleans pack, Maddox Ward, led the largest shifter pack in Louisiana, comprising a myriad of shifters, not just wolves. His beta was a tiger known for being lethal in battle. Seth Richards led a pack in Shreveport, and Travis Breaux was alpha of the Lafayette pack. Each man had their beta with them.

While Rafe knew all the men present, other than the Landry brothers, none were what he would call friends. They met up once, maybe twice a year for meetings, bringing each other up to date on issues within the state. They'd decided years ago to stand together, combining forces, to keep the Louisiana shifter's secret safe from humans.

"I'm glad you called this meeting, Martin." Maddox Ward started. "Though I'm sorry it was because of such a huge loss." He inclined his head at Sam. "It seems this drug is infiltrating into our packs in nefarious ways." His nostrils flared as he spoke. "Some of my teenage pups were approached by strange shifters. No one thought to question their identity because my pack is large and mixed."

"Are your pups all right?" Sam asked, hands clenching into fists on the table. "Moonburst is quite lethal."

"One of them, a seventeen-year-old boy, overdosed and is in a coma. Our healer isn't sure he'll survive. It was enough to scare the others to come to me and confess what had happened."

"Were you able to find the two dealers?" Rafe asked.

"Unfortunately, no," Maddox stated sadly. "But I have this." His beta handed him a folder, and he pulled out two sheets of paper. "One of the girls in the group is quite a talented artist. She sketched these for me, and I made copies for all of you." They passed the drawings around, and everyone studied them carefully.

"They don't look familiar to me," Seth said. "But I'll make sure everyone in my pack gets a look at them."

"Same here," Travis agreed. "We need to stop this before it gets any further."

Rafe looked over at Ridge. The shifter never had a lot to say, but when he spoke, people sat up and paid attention.

"Ridge, you got anything on your end?" Rafe asked.

The Cajun shifter shook his head slowly. "No, I haven't seen them, just the result of what the drug can do to a pack." He met the curious looks of the other Alphas. "I have given sanctuary, like Rafe has, to a few of Sanders' pack."

Seth looked at Sam curiously. "Aren't you keeping your pack together?"

"The women requested sanctuary from Rafe while Sanders was still Alpha." Sam's eyes flashed, but he quickly gained control of his wolf. "I won't force anyone to stay where they are not comfortable. Rafe and I discussed it, and both agreed it was better to start the pack anew with willing members."

"My apologies. I didn't mean to offend." Seth waved away his words.

"Let's stay on track, gentlemen," Rafe reminded them. Seth had always been testy, trying to be *more* than the others. One day, he'd regret that attitude. On the other hand, he was proud of Sam for handling Seth's jibe so well. It was a test, one he'd passed.

"For now, we need to get the word out—to our packs and other shifters about these dealers. They need to be apprehended, not killed outright. We need to get to the source, so we can eradicate this drug before its damage is widespread," Rafe declared.

"I agree with Martin," Maddox said. "We don't have time to waste on this one. I suggest we stay in close touch. If we work together, we can flush these two out."

It was unanimous, Rafe saw with great relief. He was hoping for such a result, but one never knew with so many alphas in one room.

"If you gentlemen would like to step outside, my men have been grilling all morning. We can fix our platters and bring them back in here to eat and relax before you head home."

"I was sincerely hoping that was for us," Maddox said appreciatively. "The delicious aroma was going to make it hard for me to just walk by."

"There's plenty." Rafe assured. "Let's make sure you get a generous helping,".

Rafe felt all his tension wash away when he spotted Lyric with the others around the grills. She was laughing with the other women, her hair spilling about her shoulders like a golden waterfall. She smiled when she looked up and saw him.

"Who's the little omega, Martin? You've been hiding the good ones?" Seth sneered.

"She's mine, Richards. Back off," Rafe warned. His hackles rose as a low warning growl rumbled from deep in his chest. The last thing he wanted was a challenge, but he would tear Seth Richards apart if he insulted his mate.

Seth looked from Lyric to Rafe, then back again at Lyric, who was nervously fidgeting.

"She's not claimed, and she's an omega. That puts her on the table, am I right?"

Maddox sidled up to the young alpha with a cautioning reproach. "If an alpha says the woman is his, you take him at his word." He raised a brow, "You may be alpha, but you're not a very smart one."

"Why, you..."

Ridge laid a large hand on Seth's shoulder, his voice a low rumble, the Cajun accent soft and easy, lessening the severity of his words. "Part of being a good alpha is knowing not to press issues when you're on another's territory. It also helps to keep you alive."

The young alpha's face was tight with rage, but he had too much pride to leave before the others. With a jerk of his shoulder, he escaped Ridge and headed for the group to get his food.

The others followed, watching him closely. Rafe, most of all. Approaching the group, Rafe met Lyric's gaze, and she hurried to his side. Draping an arm around her, he inhaled her sweet scent. Once again, the tension washed away, and he found himself able to deal with Seth Richards and any other hurdle coming his way.

Maddox stepped up, offering a hand to Lyric. "Maddox Ward, NOLA pack. It's a pleasure to meet Rafe's mate."

Lyric flustered but caught herself and shook the Alpha's hand. "Lyric Taylor, it's nice to meet you."

Maddox stared at Lyric, then turned a wide grin on Rafe. "You found yourself a Legacy, Martin? Congratulations! Those are rare indeed." He included Lyric in his beaming smile. "My best to the both of you. May you live long and happy lives."

Rafe knew Lyric was uncomfortable with the attention, but to her credit, she accepted the alpha's congratulations graciously. He should have realized Maddox Ward would know about the Omega Legacy. The size and different shifters in his pack meant he had to be knowledgeable of all their lore.

Lyric slipped away, returning quickly with a platter loaded with the choicest of cuts for Rafe. He accepted it, knowing he'd speak to her later. Rafe didn't want Lyric waiting on him. That was part of her past he wanted her to leave behind, but like many other things, it would take time. Instead, he kissed her tenderly, thanking her.

The alphas returned to the lodge with their meals, the overloaded platters lightening moods. Even Seth was eyeing his food eagerly.

"If I'm not out of line, may I ask a question?" Ridge asked. At Rafe's nod, he continued, "Maddox mentioned the Omega Legacy. I must admit I'm not familiar with it. What exactly is it?"

"May I?" Maddox asked Rafe. Again, a nod from Rafe. He had a feeling the NOLA alpha could not only explain it better, but it would also be delivered without the edge of aggression the Shreveport alpha would waken in Rafe.

With deliberate casualness, Maddox Ward wiped his hands, then took a long drink. He turned to Ridge, deliberately ignoring Seth, who was sitting on the other side of the Cajun.

"Births of a Legacy are few and far between, as you can well imagine. There probably aren't a handful alive at any one given time. Legacies are always omegas, born with unique gifts that come into fruition upon being claimed by an alpha."

"If my understanding is correct, Rafe hasn't claimed her yet. How is it you recognized her as a Legacy?" Ridge asked.

"Did you notice a sense of calming wash over us when she stepped closer to Rafe?"

"That was her doing?" Travis asked.

"It was indeed," Maddox answered. "Legacies have the gift of calming the entire pack just by their presence. She keeps them spiritually peaceful, which in turn, makes for a very contented pack. Legacy omegas nurture their people and are incredible healers. It's said the Goddess bestows the Omega Legacy only on the worthiest of alphas."

Even Seth seemed impressed with Maddox's story. He caught Rafe's eye and offered an apology. "I'm sorry, Martin. I had no idea, and I was totally out of line."

Surprised, Rafe accepted the apology for what it was. Who knew? There might be hope for the young alpha, after all.

The rest of the afternoon was spent pleasantly as the alphas got to know each other a little better. The beginnings of real friendships were formed, ensuring the Louisiana shifters a tight-knit bond.

Chapter 12

Lyric nervously paced in her bedroom; she wasn't sure exactly what had happened earlier with the other alphas. Though most of them had been quite polite, the one called Seth had reminded her of Sanders and his men, crude and offensive, at least until Maddox Ward and Ridge Landry had stepped in. She was relatively sure they had been quietly holding Rafe back from attacking the younger alpha.

Twisting her fingers, she prayed it wasn't something she'd done. The last thing she wanted was to anger Rafe. A light rap on her doorjamb made her jump, Rafe stood, silently watching her.

"Can I talk to you?"

Lyric nodded dumbly, gesturing for him to come in.

"I want to apologize for what happened earlier. Seth was out of line and if not for Maddox and Ridge, I would have started something that would have ended badly." He scratched at his beard, letting out a heavy sigh. "Seth later apologized, but it should have been to you, not me."

Lyric was stunned. Alphas didn't apologize, especially to omegas, yet that's exactly what Rafe had just done. He'd shown her a vulnerability, which was unheard of. The more she learned of Rafe Martin, the more she cared for him as a man.

"You don't owe me an explanation, much less an apology—" She never finished the sentence.

"You deserve both." Rafe pushed the hair back from her face, staring deep into her eyes, his own blazing amber. "You are my mate and deserve only respect and honor. No one will ever disrespect you again, especially in my presence. I swear it!"

Lyric lifted a shaky hand and caressed his cheek, his beard softer than what it appeared. He closed his eyes, leaning into her palm.

"I'm so sorry. All this could have been avoided if I had claimed you, but I promised I wouldn't rush you." He opened his eyes slowly, the amber receding to warm chocolate. "I'm trying, but it's not easy."

Lyric met his gaze, seeing nothing but raw and honest emotion. This man... this alpha, cared for her and cared deeply. His wolf—and her wolf—for that matter—had acknowledged each other as Fated Mates. Their beasts were never wrong. She reached up and kissed him.

Taken by surprise, Rafe stiffened but only for a second. Sweeping her into his embrace, he deepened the kiss she'd started. His tongue sought entrance, and she gave it willingly. Strong hands fisted her hair, but it wasn't like the others. It was passionate—a need without pushing or punishing. His soft groan against her neck sent a current to her core, making her come alive for the first time. Rafe's touch was like no other, and she wanted more. She wanted to know what it felt like to be loved... by Rafe.

He ended the kiss, his fingers lingering on her face. His forehead touched hers, and his breath was warm on her face.

"Let's go sit up front or better yet, outside. I can't trust myself right now. I won't lie. I want you too much."

Lyric took a deep breath, garnering her courage.

"What if I wanted you to claim me now?"

Rafe was silent for too long, rubbing the back of his neck, staring at the ceiling. Once again, Lyric was nervous she'd said the wrong thing.

"Little one, I'm not saying you don't know your own mind, never that, but I made you a promise, and I intend to keep it." He took her by the hand, leading her to the living room. Pulling her down beside him on the couch, he still held her hand.

"Lyric, if I do one thing right in my life, it's going to be this. We're both being pulled by our wolves and by the Claiming. We've accepted it, and both want it, but I'm going to tell you what I don't want." He looked so deeply into her eyes, there was no turning away.

"I never want you to cry out in fear because something I did or said reminded you of those others." He held a finger to her lips, seeing she was about to protest. "Don't say it won't happen because it could, and I'm not willing to take that chance. I'm not saying we wait long, maybe only a week or more, but I want you to be comfortable around me. I don't want you to second-guess yourself, wondering if you said the wrong thing." He caught her flinch.

"That, right there. That's what I'm talking about. I want you to know me... really know me. I want you to believe me when I tell you how much you mean to me. When we get to that point, I'll claim you." He teased her lips with a kiss.

"I'm not a young wolf, Lyric. To be honest, I didn't think I'd ever meet my mate, much less a Fated one, but here you are. My feelings for you run deep, and that's only going to get stronger. When I tell you I love you, I want you to believe me."

"I'm trying, Rafe. I want to make you proud."

"I *am* proud of you, little one." Her heart swelled with emotion when he smiled at her so tenderly. "I want you to be comfortable... with me and in your own skin. I want to know the Lyric who hasn't been allowed to be herself."

Rafe meant every word he'd told Lyric, but the waiting part would be the hardest thing he'd ever done. His wolf wasn't happy with him, constantly snarling and baring his teeth. He didn't understand what they were waiting for. Lyric was their mate, and he wanted to claim her. Simple black and white—only it wasn't. There were so many shades of gray stuck in the middle, and Rafe was trying his best to navigate them all.

He knew Lyric was trying to change for him, and that was the crux of it. He wanted her to change for herself, and odds were, she wouldn't know how to even begin. Since she'd hit puberty, she'd been treated as a servile omega. She didn't know any other way.

He was going to talk to Dottie and Miriam. They'd helped the younger girls. Maybe they could help all of them, including Lyric. A woman's get-together or something... whatever women did when they were together. Rafe was out of his element, but he was smart enough to acknowledge the fact and seek help.

"I'm going to get something to drink. Can I get you something? Wine?"

Lyric started forward. "I can get it for you."

He held out a palm, stopping her from getting up.

"Lyric, I'm perfectly capable of waiting on myself. I offered to get you something. Sit back and relax. Now, what can I get for you?" She was trying, he'd give her that, but his little omega was a bundle of nerves.

"Some wine would be nice, thank you."

"Much better." He gave her a crooked grin. Returning a few minutes later with a tumbler of whiskey and a glass of wine, he sat next to her. "See, that wasn't so hard, was it?" He took a sip of the amber liquid, watching her from the corner of his eye. The play of emotions running across her face was priceless. He finally sat back and shook his head. "Lyric, it's all right. This is what I've been talking about." He rubbed a palm up and down her thigh. "Relax."

"I'm trying." Lyric giggled into her wine.

Rafe waggled his brows at her.

She snorted.

That did it. They both burst into laughter. Rafe briefly closed his eyes. It was going to be all right.

Rafe's cell phone ringing jarred their quiet conversation. Seeing the familiar name of one of his pack, he answered.

"Rafe? George Anders."

He stood, gesturing to Lyric he'd take the call outside. She nodded in understanding, and he stepped out onto the porch.

"What can I do for you?" George owned and ran a very profitable diner downtown. Rafe had no idea why the man was calling him.

"A couple of the new women applied at my diner for work today."

"Is there a problem, George?"

"Well, that's why I'm calling you." The man sounded unsure of himself. "Lyric was one of them, and the way I understand it, she's your mate."

"She is, but I'm not seeing how this is a problem."

"I, uh, I didn't want to do anything you didn't approve of."

"She's a grown woman, George. She makes her own decisions."

"But she's your mate."

"She is, and I don't tell her what to do." Rafe lowered his voice, stepping off the porch. "These women have had a hard go of it. It's up to us to help them, and one of those ways is to instill confidence. My advice to you is if you want Lyric to work for you, call her and offer the job."

"I'll do that. She has a lot of experience. I want to offer her the manager position. That's okay with you, Alpha?"

Rafe snickered. "You're asking the wrong person."

"Right, right. I'll call her right now."

"Goodnight, George."

Rafe heard a cell phone ringing inside and Lyric's soft voice answering. Figuring he'd give her a few minutes of privacy, he stayed outside. Fall leaves swirled in a chilly wind, and a silvery crescent moon hung high in the sky. Another couple of weeks and his pack would gather for a full moon run.

He wondered if Lyric would be his mate by then. Pinching the bridge of his nose, he silently chastised himself. One day at a time. He wouldn't rush her, no matter how much his wolf growled at him.

His front door opened, the back light throwing a halo of light around Lyric's curvy frame. She bounded off the porch, across the yard, and into Rafe's arms.

"I got a job! I start tomorrow!"

"You did? Tell me about it." A smile tugged on Rafe's lips.

"You don't have to pretend," Lyric said with a sly smile. "George told me he already spoke to you. He said he wanted to be honest with me up front."

"Good for him," Rafe said approvingly. "This is what you want, baby?"

"It is!" Lyric's eyes were bright with excitement, even outside in the dark. "He offered me the manager's position. It's a step-up for me. I'm a little nervous."

"You'll do just fine; I have no doubt." Rafe draped an arm around her shoulder, guiding her back into the house. "George, and his wife, Anna, are good people. If there's anything you don't understand, just ask. They want you to succeed, just like I do."

Once inside, Rafe turned Lyric in his arms and kissed her tenderly. She trembled at his touch, and he fought to control his wolf. Now was not the time. Their relationship was still fragile, and he refused to do anything that would harm it.

"You need to get some rest. Tomorrow's a big day for you. I have a small pickup out back you can use for work."

"Thank you, Rafe... for everything."

He smiled at her, feeling that now-familiar calm wash over him.

"I really think it should be me, thanking you."

Chapter 13

Lyric bounced out of bed before the alarm went off. She was giving herself plenty of time to prepare for her first day of work. Not that she required a lot since her wardrobe was extremely limited. That would be one of the first things she started on with her first few paychecks.

The women of the pack had been more than generous to her and the others, but Lyric liked being able to provide for herself. Her life had always depended on the whims of others, and she wanted to have a say-so in her own life.

Pulling her hair back in its usual ponytail, she stopped, staring at her reflection in the mirror. Slowly, she let her hair fall about her shoulders. She wasn't waiting tables anymore—she was a manager. No one would ever pull her hair again unless she allowed it. Thoughts of Rafe with his hands twisted in her hair only brought heat coursing through her—no fear, dread, or apprehension.

Applying eyeliner, mascara, and gloss was all the make-up she used. To be honest, it was all she had. She'd never bothered with more than that. Giving herself an encouraging nod, she grabbed her purse and headed toward the kitchen.

Rafe pulled out a chair when he saw her. A plate loaded with a huge fluffy omelet and a mug of coffee was waiting for her.

"Thought you might need some breakfast."

"Rafe, you didn't need to go to all this trouble."

"It wasn't any trouble. I wanted to do this for you." He gestured to the seat. "Now, sit and eat."

She ducked her head, her hair hiding the smile. He was being so sweet to her, and it was awkward for both of them. Lyric knew darn well he didn't do this for anyone else, and she was having trouble accepting everything he did for her. Rafe had been right... it would take time to get used to each other.

"I checked over the truck and pulled it around front for you." Mug in hand, Rafe sat down next to her, and laid the keys on the table. "It's nothing fancy, just a little Ford Ranger, but it's dependable. She's yours for as long as you want."

"Thank you, Rafe. I appreciate the use of your truck." Lyric was trying to figure out who was more nervous, him or her. "Is something bothering you?"

"It's my wolf." He ran a hand through his hair, then finally nodded. "He's not real keen on you leaving us."

"But Rafe…"

"I know, baby. I know you need to do this. I'm trying to get a handle on it, but you know how it is when your wolf is insisting on something else."

She knew all too well what he was talking about. Her own wolf wasn't eager to leave the safety of Rafe and his home, but she needed this job. She needed to make her own way. Rafe understood, even if their wolves didn't.

"I better go," Lyric said.

"You didn't eat…"

Lyric draped her arms around Rafe, dropping a kiss on his head. He growled, pulling her onto his lap.

"You may leave without eating more than a bite or two, but you don't leave until I kiss you soundly." He cradled her head, pushing long tendrils away from her face. "I'm going to miss you, little omega. Will you at least text me during the day?"

"I think I can manage that." She smiled up at him. "Maybe even three times."

"Watch it, woman—I may hold you to that." Rafe growled again, his eyes flashing amber, then slanted his mouth over her lips, his tongue pushing its way in, claiming hers. Rafe deepened the kiss, his hands buried in her thick hair. She moaned, and he pulled her even closer, dropping kisses on her face, his tongue licking the side of her neck.

Lyric's breath hitched as his tongue rasped her throat, his teeth lightly raking the spot where he would claim her. Her core clenched as she fisted his shirt, her breathing turning to heavy pants.

"Rafe..." Her voice was breathy. At that moment, she wanted Rafe and his wolf. She wanted him to claim her... here on the kitchen table, she really didn't care where. His hardness thrust against her core, and if he hadn't held her cradled against his chest, she'd straddle that steel shaft and ride into oblivion. He held her so close, Lyric couldn't move.

"Give me a second, baby." His breath at her ear was warm, his voice deep, gravelly, tight with need. "Please, don't move. I need to get my wolf under control."

Lyric swallowed hard, not moving. Once again, she silently thanked him for having the control to stop because, right now, she had none. Her wolf was howling in frustration, and Lyric wasn't too far behind her. They needed their mate.

Rafe's teeth raked her shoulder, and she gasped.

"What are you doing?"

"Don't move, little one. You have to trust me. Can you do that?"

With shaky hands, she pulled her hair aside, baring her shoulder for him.

"I trust you."

He didn't sink his fangs into her shoulder like she expected. Instead, he ran his tongue over the junction between her neck and shoulder. Each time his tongue lapped the spot, Rafe inhaled her scent. With infinite care, he pricked her skin with his incisors, just enough to draw blood, then lapped the spot clean, healing the mark immediately. He helped her to sit, his hands shaking as he ran them through her long hair.

"What did you do?"

"I marked you as mine. Not a full claiming, but enough that all males will know you're mine. I probably should apologize for not asking first, but..."

This time, it was Lyric who held a finger over his lips, smiling through her tears.

"I'm glad you did." She blinked away the drops. She needed to see his gorgeous, dark, liquid eyes. "I want you to know I'm ready. I want you to claim me."

The kiss was tender, it was hard, it was sweet, it was demanding. He promised her the world with that kiss and erased all doubt and fear.

"I love you, my little omega. I will spend my life cherishing you."

Lyric gasped for air, trembling in his arms. He kissed her one last time, his lips settling on her mouth.

"Go to your new job, have a great day—" he winked slyly at her, "—and think of me."

Lyric cleared her throat as she stood, reaching for the truck keys and her purse.

"We can't do this every morning. I'll never get to work."

"No promises—" Rafe smirked.

Lyric pulled into work right on time. Considering how her morning had started, she considered that a major victory. Rafe Martin was one hell of a kisser and had left her with damp panties and a yearning for much, much more.

Somehow, her world had done a complete one-eighty, and she'd been blessed with the most wonderful mate in the world. If she had to go through hell to end up with Rafe Martin, she would do it again.

George greeted her with a welcoming smile when she entered the diner.

"Anna's in the office, getting it ready for you." He pointed to a small hallway that ducked off before the kitchen. "Go on down, first door on the left."

With a nod, she hurried to the back. She peeked into the room to see a woman with long, dark hair pulled up into a messy bun, muttering to herself as she went through a box on a chair.

"Anna?"

The woman jerked her head at the sound of her name, a wide smile crossing her face.

"You must be Lyric. Come in… and please excuse the mess." She stuck a pencil in her bun, adding to the two already there. "I told myself I would have this done before you got here, but as you can see..." She waved her hands at the chaos.

"So, what are we aiming for? Maybe I can help?"

"I think you can see why I need a manager." Anna broke into helpless laughter. "George runs the kitchen, and I bake. I've got mad skills with pies, not so much with keeping track of all this."

"How about I muddle through it and see what I have?" Lyric offered.

"You'll come get me if you need anything?" Anna's eyes brightened at the prospect of escaping the small office. "I'll be in the kitchen."

"Go, bake us something special." Lyric shooed the woman from the room. "I'll yell if I need anything."

Lost in the chaos cluttering the room, Lyric lost all track of time. The smell of fresh-baked cookies tickled Lyric's nose. She inhaled deeply, groaned, and her stomach rumbled noisily. Those bites of omelet felt like it had been ages ago.

"Figured that would get your attention." Anna grinned wickedly.

"You certainly don't play fair," Lyric teased, reaching for a cookie, still warm from the oven. "These are heavenly."

"You only get one... for now. Come up front so you can eat lunch. George is fixing your plate now."

"How much do I owe you?" Lyric cringed. She didn't have a lot of cash on her.

"As if." Anna waved her question away. "It's a perk of the job. Meals are on the house. Come on before it gets cold." Anna led her to a small table along the wall. Pointing to it, she told her, "Have a seat. I'll be right back."

Before Lyric could say anything, Anna was gone. With a shrug, she sat down and waited. Before she could take in the people eating their own meals, Anna set Lyric's meal before her with a flourish.

"Hope you like good home cooking because my George is an artist."

The aroma nearly made Lyric swoon. She dug in greedily, asking Anna around a mouthful of meatloaf. "Please tell me he shares his recipes."

"Not usually,"—Anna winked—"but I bet you could coerce one or two from him."

"This is absolutely wonderful. Please thank him for me."

"I'm sure you'll get the chance yourself. If I know my George, he'll come to check on you. Gotta run. I have another batch of cookies in the oven." With a wave, she was off.

Lyric shook her head, grinning as she went back to her meal. It was a good thing shifters didn't have to watch their weight, or she'd be in trouble with this kind of cooking to look forward to every day.

"Well, well, didn't I tell you she looked familiar?"

Lyric almost choked as the nasal voice reached her. Before she could move, a tall, wiry man sat across from her while another dragged a chair next to her. A beefy hand caught her hair and pulled it back from her face.

"She had it in a ponytail when we saw her." Using her hair, he pulled her face close to his, his breath reeking of onions. "Or maybe you never saw her face. She was usually on her knees." Their laughter was loud and obnoxious.

"Let go of me," Lyric hissed through clenched teeth.

"What's this? When did the omega get some fire?"

"Bet we could make use of that, huh, Ernie?"

"There a problem here?" George asked. "You need to unhand the lady, right now."

"Mind your business, little man," the one named Ernie sneered at George. "We have business of our own with her, and I can guarantee she ain't no lady."

They laughed even louder, and Lyric felt tears of shame fall down her cheeks.

"The man said, unhand the lady. I suggest you do it now!"

"Who the fuck do you think—"

A fist crashed into the face of the one sitting across from her, then settled over the hand holding Lyric's hair, and the man cried out in pain.

"I won't repeat myself again. Let go of her hair!"

Like a released spring, he let go of Lyric's hair, and she backed away so fast, her chair went flying. Anna caught her arm, pulling her away from the men.

Kyle made short work of the pair, Riley rushing to his side with handcuffs. Lyric didn't have to guess that they were laced with heavy doses of silver. The gloves Riley wore were a dead giveaway. Riley and Thane escorted the pair out of the diner as Kyle made his way to Lyric. Anna held her tightly, her face a tight mask of fury.

"What in the hell just happened, Kyle?" Anna bit out.

"I apologize for that, Anna. Seems we had to deal with some garbage. Those were the drug dealers we had an alert on." Kyle reached out, then caught himself. "Lyric, did they hurt you? Do I need to take you home?"

Lyric dashed away the tears, daring to glance at Anna. All she saw from the woman was worry and concern, no censure.

"I'm so sorry, Anna. If you want me to leave, I will."

"Honey, none of that was your doing, and I can guarantee you that those two won't be coming back here."

"Once Rafe gets the information he needs out of them, they won't be going anywhere," Kyle rumbled in a low voice. "But I need to know you're okay. Rafe will hang me up to dry if I left here, and you aren't all right."

"You lost all your customers because of me," Lyric gasped, fresh tears streaming.

"Honey, stop right now. Every person in this diner was a shifter. I can guarantee they'll all be back within the hour. They're giving you privacy, out of respect."

Lyric looked at Anna, then at Kyle, who nodded in agreement.

"It's our way, Lyric. We took you and the others in, and that means something to us. You're our family now. We'll look out for you and be there when you need help. We know what you and the others went through, and it's never going to happen again."

"Thank you… both of you," Lyric said haltingly. "This has been a hell of a first day."

"It's been rough, I'll give you that," Kyle agreed. "Do you want me to take you home?"

"No, I'm going to stay." She drew in a deep breath. "I'm going to call Rafe and talk to him for a few minutes… if that's all right." She glanced at Anna.

"Take all the time you need." Anna hugged her quickly, then headed toward the kitchen. "I need to bake something."

"You want me to hang around until you finish talking to Rafe?"

"No, I have to do this, Kyle." She gave him a shaky smile. "You go deal with the garbage."

Chapter 14

Rafe threw his cell phone across the room, storming for the door, then pulled himself up short. Lyric assured him she was all right and wanted to stay the rest of the day. She'd begged him not to come after her, and it had taken everything in him to give his word he'd stay home. His wolf was furious with his decision. He wasn't really happy with it, either.

He walked across the room to retrieve his phone, a stream of muttered oaths marking each step, then gave a satisfied grunt to find his phone intact. Apparently, the high-dollar case had been worth the money, though he'd bitched about paying that much for a phone case. Inspecting the device and finding no cracks, he slid it back in his pocket.

The heavy knock on his door pulled him from his thoughts. Only one person knocked like that—his brother. Striding to the door, he pulled it open.

"Why aren't you at the diner, watching over Lyric?"

"Because your woman insisted she was fine. Besides, I called Danny and Steve. They're gonna hang around and make sure nothing else happens." He didn't back down from Rafe's glare. "Come with me. I brought you a gift."

"Damnit, Kyle, I'm not in the mood for games. What do you have?"

Kyle backed up a step, crossed his muscular arms across his broad chest and stared at his brother.

"You sure are pissy when your mate isn't around."

"Kyle…" Rafe growled.

"Got those two dealers for you." He gestured with a thumb. "Get in. Thane and Riley took them to the containment cells."

"Why didn't you just say so?" Rafe strode to the truck, turned, and stared at Kyle. "Well, you comin' or what?"

Kyle shook his head in resignation, pointedly closed the front door of Rafe's cabin, and headed to the truck. As Kyle aimed for a side road leading to the back of the property, he glanced at Rafe.

"When are you going to claim Lyric?"

"That's none of your business," Rafe barked.

Kyle slammed on the brakes and glared at his brother.

"That shit, right there... that makes it my business. You need to get a grip, bro. I talked to Lyric, and yeah, she was shaken up, but she was determined to stick it out. She wanted to talk to you because she was worried about *you*." Kyle gripped the steering wheel hard. "Lyric is coming into her own. You need to let her."

"I am," Rafe grumbled. "She's working, isn't she?"

"Rafe, you need to see what's happening." Kyle took a deep breath. "All of this is happening so fast. I know you and Lyric are doing your best to deal with everything, which includes the fact you're Fated Mates." He turned, facing his brother. "Your wolf is pushing you hard and clouding your thinking."

"I know," Rafe said, his voice low. He leaned back against the headrest. "I need to let him out for a run. I was hoping it could wait until the full moon, but not at the rate things are going."

"You could claim Lyric," Kyle suggested.

"I want to. That's what's making all of this so damn hard to deal with. I want to claim her, but I don't want to rush her. She needs to heal."

"I'm not saying I'm an expert on anything," Kyle ventured, "but I have a feeling claiming your omega would go pretty far in healing her. Think about it."

Rafe stared out the passenger window, raking his fingers through his beard. What Kyle said actually made a lot of sense. He had to do something and judging by how hard his wolf was pushing, he didn't have a lot of time to figure things out.

Lyric hadn't been gone more than five hours when he started getting antsy, aimlessly wandering around his cabin. It was a good-sized cabin, but not that big. He'd wanted to take a run but couldn't trust his wolf not to head into town, which would have been a disaster. There were a lot of shifters integrated into the human factor in town, but the pack's secret remained intact.

Lyric's texts were the only thing that kept him in the cabin. He'd never been like this before, and it was a side of himself he didn't really care for. The possessiveness, the need for Lyric at his side was one thing—she was his mate—but this feeling of being unsettled was rattling him. He couldn't afford to be like this. He needed to be in control, especially of his own emotions.

"I'll discuss it with Lyric when she gets home. For now, let's deal with these two. Did anyone talk to them, or did you just dump them in cells?"

"We left the questioning to you. They match the sketches, and Lyric identified both of them. I told Thane to keep them separated. I wasn't taking any chances."

Kyle rolled to a stop in front of a dilapidated cabin that looked like it had been abandoned for years, which is exactly what Rafe had in mind when they built it three years ago—everything about the exterior was a façade. Sliding a panel up, Rafe punched in the security code. The door clicked open, and Rafe and Kyle stepped inside.

The front room had a couch, two armchairs, a table, and four chairs. They crossed the room to another door, repeating the security code process. This door opened to a completely different scene. Two cells, each six feet by eight feet, stood against the back wall. Each steel bar of the cells was fortified with silver, able to contain any shifter.

Rafe stood in front of the two cells, rolling his shoulders.

"So, you're the one." One of the men in the cell laughed suddenly. "Looks like the omega whore got herself claimed."

"You will shut your mouth about my mate, or you won't live to say another word," Rafe growled, seething with fury as his muscles tensed, veins cording down his arms. His wolf was barely restrained, so he knew his eyes were glowing a bright amber.

"Oh, I don't know about all that. Between Chuck and me, we've sampled her charms a few times. I can see why you'd want that for yourself."

Fangs punched through Rafe's gums and claws broke through his fingertips. Growling, he lunged at the caged man. Thane and Kyle rushed at him, using all their strength to hold him back.

"Rafe, think!" Kyle hissed. "You're letting them get to you!"

Rafe shrugged off Kyle and Thane as if they were petty nuisances. Claws and fangs retracted slowly, and amber irises receded back to dark brown. Rafe took a deep breath.

Easing to the man in the first cell, Rafe tilted his head. "I have no use for you. Chuck will tell me what I need to know." He spun on his heel and eyed Thane, "Get rid of that one. I've had enough of him."

Before Rafe or Thane made a move, the man realized his mistake.

"Wait! Hold on a minute," he cried. "Let's make a deal. We can talk…"

"A deal?" Rafe glared at him coldly. "Do you really think I want to make a deal with the likes of you? All I want is the name of your supplier. I want to know who's pushing Moonburst to shifters."

"I can't tell you that. He'll kill me!"

"We're already dead," Chuck said quietly. "At this point, we can only hope to die quickly." He stood and looked straight at Rafe. "Holloway, Thaddeus Holloway is the name you want. He's a vamp, up in Chicago. Got a vendetta against all shifters. He hired a bunch of freelancers like me and Mike to push the stuff."

"Why you two? You're shifters," Rafe asked.

"Didn't ask." Chuck shrugged. "The money was good, and the perks were better."

"Where in Chicago?"

"My wallet," Chuck said slowly, "I have a card in my wallet."

Rafe jutted his chin at Thane, and the enforcer eased up to the cell. Chuck rifled through his wallet and handed a card through the bars to Thane, who passed it over to Rafe.

Sanction Noir, The Columns, Chicago, Illinois. The phone number was listed at the bottom.

Rafe stuffed the card in his pocket, then motioned to Kyle.

"Deal with them. Show Chuck mercy—make it quick."

Rafe left the room and decided to walk back to his cabin. He needed the time to calm the rage tearing at him from within. He'd lost it. He'd well and truly lost it, and it wasn't acceptable, no matter how he looked at it.

Making the last corner to his cabin, he saw the Ranger parked in front. Lyric was home. Sprinting for the door, he didn't stop until he'd cleared the porch and was inside. The scent of wild roses led him to her room—the sound of running water in the bathroom stopped him short. Breathing heavy, he leaned on the doorjamb. She was taking a shower, so he didn't dare go in. His wolf, however, didn't see a problem. The water turned off and her soft voice reached him.

"Rafe? Is that you?"

"Yeah…" He cleared his throat. "It's me. I'll be up front." He turned and hurried to the living room. He couldn't trust himself. What had he been thinking when he invited her to his home? Yeah, well, a few days ago, he'd been thinking semi-clearly. All that was out the window now.

Lyric's scent made Rafe turn around slowly. Standing barefoot by the couch, wearing a fitted t-shirt and shorts, her still-damp hair hung down to her waist. She posed nervously, and Rafe fought not to scare her.

"Lyric…" Before he could say more than her name, she rushed into his arms. Plunging his hands into her hair, Rafe claimed her mouth like a dying man needing air. Wave after wave of calm rolled over him, and for the first time since early that morning, Rafe could breathe.

He crushed Lyric against him, never wanting to let her go. Rafe's hands roamed Lyric's body, convincing himself she was finally where she belonged. Pushing her hair back from her face, he tucked it behind her ear, and his tongue rimmed the delicate shell.

"I don't think I can stop, baby girl—" Rafe was on fire—he needed Lyric. This gentle, beautiful creature was the only one who could save him from himself.

"I don't want you to stop, Rafe."

Lyric's breath came in hitches and gasps as he kept up the assault of kisses. His hands never stopped, memorizing each soft curve he touched. Caressing the side of her breast, he cupped the full mound, then raised her shirt and pulled the thin strap aside with his teeth, exposing the round breast. He ran his tongue around the peaked nipple, taking it into his mouth and suckling gently. Lyric gasped, arching into his mouth as she pulled him closer.

"You need to be sure because if I take you to my bed, I'm claiming you." He groaned into her hair, deeply inhaling her shampoo and natural scent. His hands shook as he cupped her face, searching her eyes. "You need to tell me now."

"I want you to claim me."

Scooping her into his arms, he headed for his bedroom. He was claiming his mate.

Chapter 15

Rafe gently laid Lyric on the middle of his king-sized bed. Shrugging out of his clothes and boots, he tossed them aside and crawled across the sheets to settle next to Lyric. He yearned to touch every part of her, to taste her secrets. She leaned against his chest with a sigh of contentment, and at that moment, Rafe realized everything good in his world was lying beside him.

He ran his fingers through her long hair, marveling at how soft and thick it was, the silky tresses flowing through his hands. Filling his hands with her hair, he cradled her head as he kissed her tenderly, slowly deepening the kiss. When she parted her lips, he explored her mouth, her tongue meeting his. He eased her shorts off, dropping them off the edge of the bed.

His hands roamed her body, cupping her breasts, then smoothing over her stomach and resting on the patch of tight curls covering her sex. He ran a finger between her folds, and she sighed, opening her legs for him. Rafe rested his head on her stomach as he slid his fingers inside her. Her arousal spiked his desire as he stroked and petted her, listening to her gasps and sighs.

Wedging his broad shoulders between her smooth legs, he finally tasted what he'd been thinking about for days. She tensed, and he stopped, then rubbed her thighs and crooned softly to her until she relaxed enough for him to start again. His tongue worked her wet center, and this time, her moans were of pleasure. She writhed and arched against his mouth, her fingers raking through his hair as he circled her wet bud. His name came out on a long breath, and Lyric's body trembled and shuddered. He was relentless, wanting this orgasm to shatter her in all ways, wiping out the horrors of her past, making his love for her the only thing she would ever need.

Lying beside her, Rafe pulled her into his arms. He stroked her back, and her shirt rode up from the movement. She froze as Rafe felt the uneven ridges crisscrossing her back.

"Please Rafe, don't."

"Baby, I want to see. Show me."

Lyric slowly sat up, her eyes welling with tears as she pulled off the shirt. Turning, she exposed her back to him.

Rafe closed his eyes. What she must have suffered at the hands of Sanders and his men.

"They're so ugly. I knew you'd be repulsed when you saw them."

"There is nothing repulsive about you." He wrapped her in his arms, holding her tight. "You are beautiful and perfect."

"But I'm not..." she sobbed. "I'm disfigured, and no amount of shifting will ever heal the scars."

Rafe coaxed her to lie down on her stomach, then gently ran his finger along each scar. He left a trail of kisses on each ridge and welt that marred her otherwise perfect skin. His anger at Sanders threatened to rise, his wolf snarling in rage, but he forced it aside. Showing Lyric that none of it mattered was more important. She was his priority. He would never get justice from a dead man.

Turning her onto her back, he nuzzled her neck, his tongue trailing a path to the spot where he would claim her as his Fated Mate. His wolf chuffed, eager to claim her now, but Rafe forced him back, once again. He would do this his way. Lowering his mouth to hers, his kisses began softly, then built in intensity as he ravished her body with kiss after kiss. Parting her legs, he knelt between them, stroking himself, harder than he could ever remember being.

"You are so beautiful, Lyric. I wish you could see yourself through my eyes."

His shaft teased her folds, rubbing without entering, coating himself with her wetness. Lyric's breaths were heavy and uneven as he slowly entered, an inch at a time, giving her time to adjust to his size. She was tight, fitting around his length like a velvet glove. Her hips rose to meet him, and he pushed himself into the heated core of her body. Lyric cried out his name, her nails digging into his shoulders.

Rafe thrust hard and fast, and together, they found their rhythm. They made sounds without words, noises of pure pleasure. The need to explode built in him, but Rafe fought to hold on, straining his body and fighting the rush that continued to build, higher and hotter.

Lyric's body shuddered as he felt the orgasm ripple through her. With a growl of pleasure, he exploded deep inside of her. His fangs punched through, and he sank them deep into the curve of her neck. Lyric groaned in pleasure, her nails raking his arms and back. Lapping the blood, Rafe licked the punctures clean. The mark would remain.

"Your turn, baby." He offered his neck to Lyric. With trembling hands, she reached for him, her fangs punching through and slicing deep. He hissed in pleasure, encouraging her. She drank of him, then licked the mark clean, her claim lasting their lifetime together.

Pulling her into his arms, he held her close with his leg draped over hers. The mate bond opened, and the magic of Fated Mates filled their hearts and souls. Rafe could feel Lyric's heartbeat, her blood pumping steadily through her body, he knew her thoughts and feelings, and he could feel her love for him—strong, steady, and true.

"Rafe?" She turned wide eyes on him. "What's that?"

"The sound of drumbeats?" He chuckled.

"Yeah, it's getting louder, and… it's sort of spreading."

"That's the pack, baby. You're the Alpha's mate and share my link. Everyone in the pack is linked to you now."

"Is it always going to be this loud?"

"It'll subside in a minute or two. You'll get used to it. After a while, it'll be a warm feeling in your heart. If anyone gets seriously hurt or in trouble, you'll feel it." He kissed her temple. "The pack is a lot of responsibility, but the Goddess knew what she was doing when she sent you to me. I love you, Lyric, and I will spend the rest of our lives together showing you how much I care."

Lyric's blue eyes filled with tears, but this time, they were tears of joy. She played with the dusting of hair on his chest.

"I can't tell you how much you mean to me, Rafe. You've changed my life and shown me a love I never knew I could have. I'll always love you."

Holding her tightly in his arms, they drifted off to sleep. Hours later, she woke to his kiss, his shaft heavy with need once more. She welcomed him into her arms, and he made love to his mate again.

Rafe sat back in the old rocking chair, his jeans sitting low on his hips and his flannel shirt unbuttoned, with a mug of coffee warming his hands as he watched the sunrise. He couldn't remember ever feeling so at peace with everything in his world. There were still things to be taken care of, but it would all get done, in time.

The door opened, and Lyric stepped onto the porch, holding her own mug of coffee. She'd traded her t-shirt and shorts for jeans and one of his flannel shirts. The November morning held a definite chill in the air.

"Mind if I join you?"

"Didn't want to wake you, but I was hoping for your company." Rafe patted the empty rocker next to him.

"Did you sleep well, baby girl?" he asked as Lyric settled in next to him.

"I did." She smiled contentedly. "When you let me sleep," she teased.

"Are you complaining?"

"Nope, not one bit."

They rocked in silence for a few minutes, sipping coffee and enjoying the beauty of the sunrise and the peaceful quiet of the early morning.

"I love this weather," Rafe broke the silence. "It's going to make for a perfect full moon run." He reached for her hand. "I look forward to running with my mate."

Her bottom lip quivered for a moment, then she smiled shyly. "I never thought I would ever have a mate to run with."

"You do now, and you always will." He placed tender kisses on her knuckles, refusing to let go of her hand.

"Rafe?"

"Hmm?" His head rested against the back of the chair, his eyes closed in contentment.

"Are you going to let me go back to work?"

Opening his eyes, he set his mug down, and gently squeezed her hand.

"As long as you want to work, you can. I don't have a problem with you holding down a job. The problem yesterday was my wolf—he's been pushing me hard to claim you, and it was driving both of us over the edge. Now that you belong to us, the bond is open, and we'll know at all times if you're all right."

"As for the other, the dealers who sold to Sanders are a thing of the past. I got the supplier's name and where he's located out of one of them. I'm calling Maddox today and filling him in. Ward has the largest pack in Louisiana, and with his different shifters, he has the manpower to send out to deal with this guy."

"Just for the record, I don't want you to get mad at me if my boys drop in at the diner from time to time." His voice dropped lower as his emotions surged. "I'm never going to take a chance of anything happening to you ever again. Anna and George are good people, but they're not fighters."

"Do you think we're still going to have problems with the supplier?"

"I hope not, but for now, we're not taking any chances."

"I guess I can live with that." Lyric sat back, sipping her coffee, then tilted her head, a smile curving her lips. "You sure seem content right now."

"Going to be like that from now on," he replied. "It's you, baby girl. This is the Omega Legacy. Now that I've claimed you, your gifts will spread to the entire pack, and they'll feel what you send out. Crossroads is going to be a very special pack, thanks to you."

The End

Before You Go!

If you liked this book, please do me a huge favor, and leave a review. Reviews are a small thing that mean so much to authors. They're invaluable as a means of advertising.

Thanks in advance!

Madison Granger
AUTHOR

Phoenix Rising

Book One of The Kindred Series

———————

Madison Granger

Chapter 1

Torie conceded to two thoughts simultaneously; Christmas shopping was overrated, and the spirit of Christmas was dead, buried under a glittering blanket of commercialism. She'd never been a big fan of crowds. There were way too many people out and about this weekend for her liking. She was doing her best to forge through the masses to get the last elusive gift items on her list. Then there was the traffic. "Seriously! Does everyone think they have the only vehicle on the road?" she muttered. It seemed the streaming multitude left their IQ's and common sense at home. If she made it to her house in one piece, she would consider herself a holiday shopper survivor.

Torie parked her SUV, sighing with resignation for the things she couldn't control. Grabbing her cell phone, keys, and purse, she headed across the full parking lot to the local bookstore. She'd been out all morning and most of the afternoon in search of Christmas presents for friends. Usually, she shopped online, but sometimes you just had to get out and fight the crowds for that *perfect* gift. Unfortunately, those *perfect* gifts were getting harder and harder to find, or someone else had the same idea and by the time Torie got to the shelf, they were already gone. Frustration was rearing its ugly head. She'd come to the realization that she needed an indulgence break before continuing her search. A book for herself and a shot of caffeine should brace her for the rest of the shopping day.

Entering The Literal Word, she was regaled with bright lights, colorful displays, and Christmas music playing over the speakers. Torie loved this store. She delighted in the convenience of shopping online, but there was nothing like browsing aisles and shelves of books.

Here, she was in her element. Books were her comfort zone, her friend, and her solace when she needed mental pampering. As she glanced around the setup, Torie took in the crowd browsing for books or the latest book-related gadget. There were plenty of them. People were running into each other trying to get through narrow passages to look at all the items.

Java Joe's, the in-house coffee shop, was also catering to a maximum crowd. Wistfully, Torie wondered if she would be able to get a cappuccino after she'd made her purchases. Slinging her bag up on her shoulder, she navigated to her favorite section. A romance book with a sexy werewolf or vampire was always a welcome escape from her busy, but lonely life. An auburn-haired, green eyed middle-age divorcee, Torie was a graduate of the *been there, done that, have a drawer full of t-shirts* school of life. After so many failed relationships, she was pretty sure the rest of her life was going to be spent alone. Being on the more-than-curvy side pretty much insured it. Men her age seemed to all want that pretty, young trophy type on their arm. *It is what it is* had become her mantra.

It wasn't a bad life, in itself. Torie had family, a brother and sister. She also had a grown daughter and a precocious granddaughter she adored. She had a job she liked, and made a decent living, too. There just wasn't a special man in her life. That kind of loneliness was hard for her. It had been a long time since there had been anyone memorable. Torie missed the best parts of a relationship, the companionship, sharing of ideas and thoughts, laughter, and the sex. *Yeah, I miss the sex.* Shaking her head ruefully, she berated herself for the pity party. That kind of thinking was depressing and never got her anywhere. It was time to shove it back into that tiny compartment in her brain and try, once again, to forget about it.

Approaching the Paranormal Romance section, Torie noticed they'd added a tier of shelves right before it of New Releases. *Well, this makes it a little easier to find what I'm looking for.* Browsing through the titles, she scanned for releases by her favorite authors first. Torie picked up a few unknowns and started reading the back covers to find her next book boyfriend. After selecting a couple that seemed promising, she ambled over to another section of her favored genres, Science Fantasy. There was one book that had been released recently. She wondered if it was on the shelf yet, or if she would have to order it.

When she got to the section, Torie spotted her goal on a lower shelf. *Naturally! Why do they have to put them way down there?* Bending down, she grabbed the book. As she straightened, she lost her balance and faltered side to side, dropping everything. Her purse too, fell off her shoulder, landing on the floor. Reddening with embarrassment, Torie bent down to retrieve her goods with a muttered oath. A man's strong, long-fingered hand came into her line of vision, reaching for her books as Torie grabbed her purse.

"Allow me," entreated an amused deep voice. He held her arm, lending her his support so she could stand.

Flustered beyond belief, still blushing furiously, Torie peered up to thank the man for his kindness. She gazed into the most mesmerizing pair of sky-blue eyes she'd ever seen. Torie found herself struck dumb. She took in his shaved head, a handsome face with a sexy soul patch under his bottom lip, and a drop-dead killer smile. She finally managed to stammer, "Tha . . . thank you."

He smiled back at her. "Always a pleasure to assist a lady in distress."

The handsome stranger held the books out to her. Torie, regaining her composure, reached up to take them back into her arms. She couldn't help but notice how very tall he was. She looked up to give him a grateful smile. His tailored slacks and button-down shirt did nothing to disguise the definition of his well-sculpted body. The rolled sleeves partially covered what appeared to be a full sleeve of tribal tattoos on his right arm. *Oh my, this guy is the stuff fantasies are made of.*

His gaze went from her arms loaded with books to making eye contact. "Have you found everything you are looking for?" His smile, devastatingly sexy, was aimed right at her. Her heart went into overdrive. It'd been ages since she found herself attracted to any man, and here was her proverbial *sex on a stick,* talking to *her.* She said a quick prayer not to flub this. "Yes, as far as shopping for books goes, I'm pretty well done."

"In that case," he started in a low pitched, husky voice, "could I interest you in a coffee?"

Torie double-checked to see if he was indeed serious in his offer. The expression on his face seemed sincere. There was no way she was going to pass up on this chance to find out who this gorgeous guy was. Her mouth curved into a smile. "I'd love some coffee.

Thanks. Let me pay for my books first, and I'll meet you there."

Sweeping an arm out toward the front of the store, he motioned for her to go first. As she turned to go to the registers, he added, "I shall wait for you here."

Throwing him a quick smile, she got in line hoping it wouldn't take long to pay for her books.

For once, they had enough employees behind the counters. Checkout went quickly and she met up with him. Walking toward the coffee shop, her handsome Good Samaritan leaned toward her. "What kind of coffee would you like?"

Torie always got flustered trying to make decisions at these coffee places. There were so many to choose from and she never could decide what she wanted. Everyone else always seemed to know exactly what they desired all the time. The man asking the question now upped the ante. Looking up at the lighted sign on the wall, she noticed the highlighted special. Crossing her fingers that it was a decent choice, she answered, "The Spiced Gingerbread Cappuccino sounds interesting."

Walking to the counter to place their orders, he turned back to her. "Would you mind getting a table for us? I will be there shortly with our coffees."

As Torie glanced around the crowded room, her gaze locked on a table that was being vacated. She hurried over, cleaned up after the couple who'd left everything behind, and disposed of the trash. In the few minutes she had to wait for the handsome stranger to join her, she tried to regain her composure and get her act together. *She was acting like a schoolgirl, for crying out loud.* It had been such a long time since she had any social interaction with a man, she was sorely out of practice and nervous. As he neared the table, she once again marveled at him. He was drop-dead gorgeous. This stranger was everything she'd ever fantasized about when it came to the perfect man. Now she would find out if his personality matched the outside. She sighed. *A woman could only hope.*

He carefully placed their coffees on the table and sat across from her. The table and chairs weren't small, yet he seemed to dwarf everything around him. Not only was he a big man, but his presence also seemed to add *more* to his already dominating size. With a heart-melting smile, he introduced himself. "My name is Quinn McGrath, and you are?"

Flustered by his sensuous smile, Torie bit her lip before returning the introduction. "I'm Torie Masters. Thank you for the coffee . . . and again for your help earlier."

"Not a problem, believe me. I am glad I was in the right place at the right time."

To her relief, their conversation went smoothly. She'd never been very good at chatting. He kept the conversational flow going by asking questions and listening intently to her answers. Torie discovered that Quinn, like her, was an avid reader. He preferred mysteries and a little science fiction, having several favorite authors in both genres. From books, they ventured to movies and music. She was continually surprised at how much they had in common. The conversation between them flowed easily and the banter was light and casual, making the time pass quickly.

When Torie heard her phone chime with a text, she checked it hastily. She'd heard the faint chime a couple of times before but had ignored it. She'd been enjoying her conversation too much to want to be interrupted. Figuring her daughter was going to be persistent until she replied, she tapped out a quick answer. Looking at the clock on the face of her phone, she was astonished to find that more than two hours had passed. She noticed a slight look of disappointment flitting across Quinn's handsome face as she checked the messages. She looked up when he enquired, "Do you have to go?"

"No, not at all. My daughter is checking on me. I'm not usually out this long," she confessed.

"Excellent. Could I persuade you to have dinner with me? I am enjoying your company and I really am not ready for our time together to end."

Torie's initial reaction was to thank him politely and decline the invitation, but she hesitated. Here was an uber attractive man who seemed genuinely interested in her. They had spent the last two hours caught up in captivating conversation. *Why **not** have dinner with him? What could it possibly hurt?* It had been way too long since she'd enjoyed the company of a man. She was going to do this.

Quinn must have understood her hesitancy. When she didn't respond immediately, he added, "I realize we do not know each other yet. There is a steak house right across the parking lot, we can walk over there to have dinner. You will not be far from your vehicle." He placed his hand over hers briefly. "Would that make you feel a little more secure?"

Didn't that just seal the deal? "I would really like that. Thank you." She accepted his invitation with a gracious smile.

Quinn cleared away their coffee cups. Coming back to the table, he reached for her purchases. "Would you like to put these in your vehicle before we go to the restaurant?"

Feeling like he was reading her mind, she readily agreed. "That would be great. My truck is right out front."

With a hand on the small of her back, Quinn escorted her out of the bookstore and to her SUV. She stashed her bag in the back with her other purchases before making sure it was locked. They walked through the still full parking lot over to Vincent's Restaurant. It was one of her favorite places to eat. The aroma of grilled steaks and freshly baked bread filled the air, greeting them before they reached the door.

Entering the dimly lit crowded eatery threw Torie's assaulted senses into overload. The dining area echoed with laughter, music, plates clanging, and murmured conversations. Trying to acclimate to the soft lighting and not get crushed by the crowd was a challenge. Quinn took charge immediately, using his body to protect her from the hordes of people rushing around them. He put an arm around her shoulders, drawing her close. It was all Torie could do not to melt right into Quinn's side. *He's so very strong . . . and rock solid . . . and his scent . . . what was that? Sandalwood, Sage, both? It was glorious, whatever it was.* She wanted to stay right where she was, drinking him in.

Quinn flashed a charming smile at the hostess, and they were quickly led to their seats. Torie wondered how that happened so fast, considering there was a group of people standing around the entrance, obviously on a wait list. She saw the young woman beaming up at Quinn, trying her best to be flirtatious. Torie smiled to herself. She couldn't blame the attendant for trying. If it got them a table, then more power to her and Quinn. Pulling out a chair for her, Quinn waited until she settled in her seat before walking around the table to take his own chair. He ran his hand lightly over Torie's shoulders as he walked by. *Brownie points for manners.* She indulged in an inward thrill at his touch, grateful she hadn't been wearing a jacket or coat that would have hampered the feel of his caress. As much as she enjoyed colder weather, the winters in southern Louisiana were usually mild.

"Is this to your liking?" asked Quinn, pulling her from her thoughts.

"Yes, it's fine," she replied, still amazed at how quickly they had been seated.

A server came up immediately to take their drink orders, leaving them for a few minutes to go over their menus, and make their choices. Finding out how akin their preferences were in other areas, it wasn't all that surprising to discover they had similar tastes in food and how it was prepared. The conversation quickly picked up where it had left off at the bookstore. She found out that he was a financial consultant and owned his own business, McGrath Consulting. His brother, who had a corporate law background, was his partner. Quinn was looking for office space in the New Orleans and surrounding areas which had led him to Torie's hometown.

Their conversation paused when the server returned with their meals. As the food was placed in front of them, Quinn assured the server that everything was fine, and the young man left them to enjoy their meal. Resuming their talk, Quinn questioned her about her job. Torie was a little abashed to admit she was just a receptionist. He was quick to quash the *just* part of her job description. When he spoke to her, she felt like she was important, that what she did counted. Torie knew he was right. She did a lot more than simply answer phones and take messages, though seldom did anyone think of it that way, especially her boss.

Over their meal, Quinn regaled her with stories of his childhood in Scotland. Torie was fascinated. She'd always dreamed of visiting Scotland but didn't think she would ever get the chance to travel. He had a way of telling stories that took her there, making her visualize the lovely scenery and the antics of two young brothers growing up in the Highlands.

"I have to say, for growing up in Scotland you don't have much of an accent," she observed between bites.

Quinn nodded. "It is true. It has faded over time. I have been away from Scotland for many years now. I have traveled the world over, several times. When you have had as many business dealings as I have with people of different cultures you tend to lose the accent. Aiming a disarming smile her way he added in a thick Scottish brogue, "Dinna fash yirsel lassie. Ah kin pull it oot whin a'm needin' it." He capped it off by throwing her a roguish wink.

"Yes indeed, you can. It's still there." Torie laughed in delight.

Later, lingering over coffee after their meal, Torie glanced around the room. It dawned on her that only a few patrons remained. "I guess we better call it a night. They'll be closing on us pretty soon."

Quinn reluctantly agreed. "Time seems to have gotten away from me today. I will walk you back to your vehicle." They wound their way through the tables, to make their way outside. Taking her hand, Quinn escorted Torie back to her truck. "Is there a chance I can see you tomorrow? I do not wish to rush you, but there is a reason for my asking."

Torie regarded him quizzically. "What do you mean?"

"I am going to be out of town for the next two weeks on business. I have really enjoyed my time with you today and I want to see you again before I have to leave," Quinn explained. "Please say yes."

"How can I possibly say no to that?" she asked, smiling brightly.

"Excellent!" Quinn replied with a broad grin. "Lunch, then?"

Laughing, Torie nodded. "Lunch, it is."

After exchanging phone numbers, Torie got into her SUV. In her rearview mirror, she could see Quinn stand in place as he watched her drive off, then slowly walk to his own car.

Torie drove home in a daze. *Who knew that today would be the stuff dreams were made of?* Parking her truck under the carport, she heard the chime that let her know she had a text message. Glancing down at her cell phone, she saw it was from Quinn.

Thank you for today. I look forward to seeing you tomorrow. ~Q.

Hugging herself, she knew she was going to have the most pleasant of dreams that night.

A Valkyrie's Vow

———————

Madison Granger

Chapter 1

Sigrid slid the platter of meat onto the table and turned to collect the empty mugs, replacing them with full ones, all the while dodging the arm of a warrior who had been in his cups for way too long. He tried to snag her by the waist, but she evaded him gracefully. Her long blonde hair was braided in an intricate pattern for more than decoration. Warriors couldn't grab her hair easily as she weaved through the tables. Her cobalt blue eyes were always alert for such obstacles.

Slipping through the back door of the kitchen, she made her way outside. Just a breather, a few minutes away from the never-ending feasting and merriment.

Sigi stared off into the distance. The sun was setting, which meant nothing in Valhalla. When she walked back into the hall, warriors would still be drinking and feasting. Never-ending, right?

"What troubles you, Sigrid?"

The voice startled her, and she whirled around.

"I... I am sorry, All Father, I didn't know you were here."

Odin chuckled lightly.

"I would be slipping in my role as All Father if you had heard me." He moved silently to her side. "I have been watching you. You are not happy, shield-maiden. How can I fix it?"

"I don't know what is wrong," she began, shaking her head.

Odin peered into her eyes.

"It's the truth, I swear it!"

The corner of his good eye crinkled as he smiled at her. He tapped the leather patch over his other eye.

"I don't need both eyes to know there is something bothering you. Though this is obviously not a job for Huginn and Muninn." He thought for a moment. "Perhaps you could use a change of scenery."

A thrill coursed through her veins at his words.

"Oh, ho! Is that it, then? My Valkyrie is bored. Perhaps a task?"

"Yes, All Father! A task, give me something to do other than serving meat and ale day in and day out." She blushed at her audacity. It slipped out, and there was no going back now.

Odin patted her hand gently.

"This, my daughter, I can do for you. Perhaps I should check on the other Valkyrie. They may want something to do from time to time as well. I shall make it my responsibility." Odin led her to a pair of chairs facing the diminishing sunset. Purple, orange, and red hues turned the evening sky to fire as they watched.

"Now, let's get back to your task. I think I have the perfect thing for you."

"You do?" Sigi looked at him in astonishment.

He chuckled. "My dear... All Father, remember?"

"Forgive me." She blushed once more.

He waved her away.

"The world has changed greatly the last few millennia. Men are not the warriors of old." He gave her a knowing look. "Perhaps that is why the Valkyrie don't leave the hall as much these days." Steepling his fingers, he sat back in the chair.

"But I digress. There is a warrior I have been watching as of late. His time is near, and I want him as one of my Einherjar, but I foresee trouble. His path is veering, and if he continues, he will have crossed over and not be worthy of becoming one of mine."

"You want me to change things?"

Once again, Odin gave her a knowing look.

"You possess the power, Sigrid. Just keep him from crossing the line. His heart is true. His mind, however, is troubled."

"I can do that for you, All Father."

Odin smiled at her. "I have no doubt. When this warrior's time comes, bring him home, my child, to Valhalla."

Sigi bowed her head, fist across her chest.

"You have my vow."

Chapter 2

Sigi stood on a dirt road next to an SUV with a flat rear tire. Turning, she took in her surroundings. Absolutely. No. One. Around. Where had Heimdall sent her? She'd gone to the Bifrost under Odin's orders. She never thought once to question either one of them.

Returning to the vehicle, she reached for the wallet on the passenger seat. She opened it and flipped through the cards—credit cards and money, lots of it. There it was... a driver's license. Sigrid Olson from Houston, Texas.

Well, she knew what name she was going by and where she was supposedly from, but it didn't answer where she was now or how she was supposed to fix a flat tire. Knowledge filled her on how to survive in this day and time but nothing about the damnable tire.

Well, she wouldn't let this stop her from achieving the task Odin had entrusted to her. There was no way she was returning to Asgard empty-handed. She would figure out how to fix the tire, find out where she was, then find her warrior—in that order.

Rifling through the glove compartment, she found an owner's manual. Scanning the pages, Sigi found the chapter, How to Change Tires. She quickly read the instructions and set about finding the tools required. Thankfully, Odin had seen fit to outfit her with a new vehicle and a spare tire.

Making a mental note to find a better jack once she had the opportunity, Sigi went about removing the flat tire. She wiped the sweat from her forehead and grimaced at the dirt on her sleeve. Wherever she was, it was hot. Her clothes were sticking to her, and she was becoming exasperated with the stupid tire. She was thirsty, too. Another pass through the truck didn't turn up as much as a bottle of water.

Sigi leaned against the SUV, scowling at the tire lying in the dust beside her. What initially had seemed to have been a good spare turned out to be good only on one side. Turning it over, she'd discovered someone had slipped a bad one on her new vehicle. One-half of the tire was thin and flimsy. How it happened was beyond her, but there it was. She didn't dare put it on the SUV. It was an accident waiting to happen.

She threw her hands up in the air. *What was she supposed to do now?*

The sound of a vehicle rumbling over the hill caught her attention. Maybe help was on the way. The truck coasted down the hill, dust roiling in great waves behind it, and finally idled to a stop near her. The truck—she was generous in the description—was as dusty as the road under her feet, but at least it was running. Focusing on the grinning man in the driver's window, she did a double take. Easy on the eyes—light brown hair, a little on the long side, three-day beard stubble, and clear blue eyes set in a kind, tanned face.

"Need some help, little lady?"

Little lady? Did that oaf truly just say that?

Sigi felt the trickling of more knowledge.

Doesn't it just figure? He's the warrior?? Are you kidding me?? Though she had to admit his drawl was pretty sexy.

She swallowed everything sarcastic and pasted on a pleasant smile.

"If you have a decent tire, which would be great. Otherwise... probably not." Sigi kicked the spare, flipping it over so he could see the problem.

"Ouch." He slipped out of the truck and winced. Crouching down, he stood the tire up, examining both sides. "How does this even happen?"

"Beats me," Sigi shrugged. "One side looks brand new, but the other side looks as old as the hills."

The man stood, scratching his head. "The garage in town doesn't have a lot on hand. Will probably have to drive to Waco." He seemed to catch himself. "I'm sorry. Slade Larsen, local rancher." He extended a hand.

"Sigrid Olson." Sigi took his hand, approving of the firm yet gentle grip. "Most everyone calls me Sigi." She tried to smile, but the heat and the start of this task were wearing on her.

"Tell you what, Sigi. Why don't you ride with me to my ranch? I'll unload my feed and groceries, then we'll call Chet at the garage about your tire."

She thought about his offer for all of two seconds.

"If there's a bottle of cold water in the deal, I'm in."

Slade laughed. "Hang on, got you covered." He leaned inside his truck, coming out with a dripping bottle of ice-cold water. "Here you go."

Sigi took a long pull on the icy liquid. There was nothing finer in Asgard. She gave him a grateful smile.

"Thanks, I needed it." She finished off the bottle and tossed it in the back seat of her vehicle. "Are there any hotels in town where I can stay for the night?"

"Fraid not," Slade answered with a shake of his head. "Broken Branch is small, doesn't even have so much as a motel or B&B, but I have room at my place. You can have one of the guest rooms."

Arching a brow, she gave him a skeptical look.

Hands raised, he went on. "Okay, I know we just met, and you don't know me from Adam, but it's all good. We won't be out there all alone. I've got the boys back at the house."

"Uh-huh, and that makes it all better?"

Slade laughed out loud. "Okay, you got me on that one. It doesn't sound good, but I swear I'm harmless. I take on homeless kids, mostly boys. It's a hard life for the girls, so they usually don't stay. The deal is they help out at the ranch, and I give them a place to stay and teach them a trade. It's worked for the last few years."

Slade tossed Sigi's suitcase into the bed of his truck, then watched as she reached inside her vehicle to grab a wallet and backpack and lock up the SUV.

The view from his end was intriguing. The blonde was curvy in all the right spots and had legs for miles. He could imagine... No, he would not imagine anything about Sigi. Reaching inside his truck, he snagged his ball cap, clamping it down on his head and turning it around, with the bill in the back. Jogging to the passenger side, he opened the door for her. He might live in the middle of nowhere, but his mama made sure he had some manners and he even used them from time to time.

Slipping into the driver's seat, he started up Ol' Betsy, giving her an affectionate pat on the dashboard as the engine roared to life.

"She ain't much to look at, but she's never let me down," he joked.

"Guess I have the wrong relationship with my vehicle."

"Stuff happens. We'll get it sorted out for you." Slade gave her a sidelong glance. "Where were you headed? There's not much out here."

Her expression shuttered, and Slade knew whatever was coming out of her mouth would be a lie. Years of experience with runaways had given him an instinct for ferreting out the truth or seeing a lie for what it was. He was seldom wrong.

Sigi opened her mouth, shut it, then stared at the low-lying hills in the distance.

"I don't know, to be honest. Figured when I got there, I'd know."

Slade pushed at his cap. Huh. That was about as honest an answer as he'd ever heard.

"Looking for something in particular?"

Sigi smiled at him, the smile open this time. "Same answer, I guess."

"Fair enough." Slade wondered about the beauty beside him. She was intriguing, to say the least. There was something about her that made him want to know her better, but it would only happen if she hung around. Way out in the middle of nowhere, what would she do with herself? Of course, there was... No, he wasn't going there. She would never go for it. Shelving the idea for later, he pulled through the arched gateway to his ranch. Driving to the back of the rustic, two-story cabin, he stopped the engine.

"Need to put away the groceries, then I'll get the boys to unload the feed. We can call Chet after."

With a nod, Sigi grabbed a couple of bags of groceries and followed him inside, glancing around the tidy kitchen as she set the bags down. Slade was glad he'd taken the time to clean up after lunch. Since Marybeth quit, they'd been taking turns cooking and cleaning. Wasn't always the best, but they were managing, and no one had died yet.

Slade brought in Sigi's suitcase and set it in the hallway, not taking for granted she would stay. Watching her unpack the groceries as if she belonged had him thinking ahead of himself once again.

The back door slammed, and the sound of exuberant teenagers filled the kitchen.

"Hey Slade, did you remember the hotdogs?"

"And the buns... last time you forgot the..."

Silence filled the room when the boys realized there was someone else in the room.

"Boys, meet Sigi Olson. She had a breakdown up the road, and I brought her here, so we could call the garage." Turning to Dean, he added, "And yes, I remembered the hot dogs." Fishing a large pack of buns from one of the bags, he tossed them to Jesús. "And here's your buns." He clapped his hands. "Line up guys, so I can introduce you proper-like."

The boys scuffled a bit but lined up against the counter according to height.

Slade pointed to the tallest. "The tall, slim one over there is Dean. He's been with me the longest and is supposed to help me keep the others in line. Doesn't always work out like that."

Dean gave Sigi a sheepish grin. "Nice to meet you, ma'am."

"Next, we have Tyler and Chase. They're not brothers, but they might as well be. They came in together."

Both boys gave her a shy smile and waved.

"Now, the quiet one there,"—he pointed at the dark-haired boy—"that's Jesús, and you have to watch him."

Jesús' eyes widened. "Man, why you want to tell the lady that? You know it ain't true!"

They all burst out in laughter.

Sigi turned to Slade, confusion marked plainly on her face.

"I told her,"—he glanced at Jesús— "because otherwise she won't believe you can speak."

Jesús' dusky skin turned ruddy.

"Just playin', hombrecito *(little man),*" Slade assured the boy, glancing at Sigi, "He can go days without saying a word. If you look up quiet in the dictionary, you'll find a picture of Jesús."

Jesús glared, but a smile broke through, showing he was used to the teasing.

Still laughing, Slade pointed to the boy on the end. "And that brings us to Nick. He's our newbie, but he's tough. Been holding his own with the rest of them."

"It's nice to meet you all." Sigi smiled at them, her manner easy and relaxed.

"Now, before you even think you're going to monopolize her time, I need you all to get down to the barn and unload the feed. While you're there, start feeding while I help Sigi with her SUV and start on supper." He tossed the keys to Dean. "Make sure they don't forget to water everybody. It's hot as Hades today, and they go through those troughs fast."

"Will do, boss."

The clamor of boots filed out the kitchen door and down the steps.

Sigi watched them leave from the window over the sink, then turned in wonder, "It's so quiet now." She laughed lightly.

"Yeah, well, they're a lot to take together, but I've gotten used to them." He fumbled for the folded sheet of paper he'd tucked in his pocket earlier.

Sigi gave him a questioning look.

"I wrote down the size of your tire, so I wouldn't get it wrong." He pulled up a chair to the phone on the wall and placed a call. As he chewed the fat with Chet, before he got down to business, he watched Sigi.

Peering into the bags, she started unpacking the groceries. Finding the pantry, she put things away. Once done, she opened the refrigerator and pulled out the pan of deer meat he'd been marinating and planned to country-fry for their supper tonight. Now he just watched Sigi, curious what she was up to.

Chet caught his attention, and he turned away from Sigi to inquire about tires. Once done with the phone call, he hung up and turned to find his guest in the midst of preparing supper.

"Uh, Sigi, what are you doing?"

She looked at him over her shoulder. "You mentioned you had to cook supper, and this was in the refrigerator, so I assumed you were going to fix this." She washed her hands, drying them on a towel as she turned to face him. "Was I wrong to start?"

He crossed the kitchen to stand in front of her.

"No, not wrong, but you shouldn't have." He winced at the hurt look that flitted across her lovely face. "You're my guest. I'm trying to help you, not the other way around."

"Who says we can't help each other?" Her cobalt blue eyes danced with humor.

"Sigi, feeding six guys is a lot of work… and a lot of food. You're going to wear yourself out."

"Why don't you let me worry about it." She rubbed his arm and pushed him into a chair. "Now, I'm guessing mashed potatoes with the country-fried steak?"

Slade stared at her in astonishment.

"Uh, yeah, that would be great."

"That's what I thought." With a chuckle, she set a bowl of potatoes on the table in front of him. "You peel."

Gambit

Madison Granger

Gam·bit

noun

A device, action, or opening remark, typically one entailing a degree of risk, that is calculated to gain an advantage.

(In chess) An opening in which a player makes a sacrifice, typically of a pawn, for the sake of some compensating advantage.

Chapter 1

Skylar Mason sat at the huge oval table, hands in her lap, unseen by the others. She tensed her fingers—claws protruding—retract—and breathe. It was an exercise in patience—either that, or she was going to clear the polished surface and tear out the throats of the nine idiots sharing the room with her.

If they used that phrase one more time...

"Skylar, you must see it's for the good of the pack."

There it was.

Skylar pushed from the table, hands splayed as she leaned over the expanse of polished wood. Emanating a small wave of Alpha power, she eyed each council member, glaring until they bowed their heads or looked away. With a smug streak of satisfaction, she addressed them.

"Members of the council, if anyone knows what is for the good of the pack, it would be me. Or have you forgotten who the Alpha is here and how long I have been Alpha?"

Daniel Cottersworth muttered under his breath, and Skylar slammed a hand on the table, the force of the sound echoing in the room.

"Daniel, if you disrespect me one more time, I will personally take you out to the fighting grounds and remind you why I am Alpha." She was so over his petty jabs and whiny attacks at her over the years. One day, she would deal with him, but unfortunately, it wouldn't be today. She didn't have the time.

The council member lowered his head, shoulders slumping.

"Forgive me, Alpha. It won't happen again."

She glared at him with the full force of her anger. She'd had enough of this nonsense and was going to shut it down for good.

"You called me in here, yet again, for the same tired tripe. For the good of the pack, I should take a mate and start a family, ensuring my line." She took another deep breath, throwing her shoulders back, every bit of her five-foot, ten-inch frame rigid. She paced the floor in her four-inch stilettos, reminding them she was taller than most of them. "And I will say again, when I get good and ready, I will take a mate. When the

Goddess blesses my mating, I will have a pup. Not. One. Day. Before. Do you understand me?"

"But Skylar, you've been Alpha for decades, yet you show no interest in any of the males of the pack. We need a Mason to continue the line."

"You realize if I take a mate, my pup will not be a Mason?"

"You know what we mean, Alpha. We need the bloodline to continue. The Mason line is the strongest of all. Your pup will carry it on, no matter the name they carry," Daniel railed.

Skylar sat back down, wondering what it would take to get through to these men.

"Haven't you realized if I show no interest in the eligible males, it's because there *is* no interest? I will *not* mate to a male I'm not interested in."

"You can't possibly be holding out for your Fated Mate? The odds of that happening are astronomical. Surely, you're not a romantic?" Louis Brennan asked incredulously.

"Sixty years, gentlemen." Skylar tapped manicured nails in a warning rhythm. "In those sixty years as Alpha, have I ever come across as weak or a sensitive romantic?" She glowered at each one of them. Once again, they shook their heads or looked away. "I thought not." Skylar sneered. "Now, if we're done here?"

She left the unspoken warning on the table. Skylar would sit right here and watch every one of them leave. It was more than stubbornness on her part. She hadn't kept her position by not paying attention. The Lunar Goddess knew she had more than enough enemies—most were known and had been dealt with, but there would always be more.

Skylar studied her nails, feigning indifference, but she watched as six council members filed out. Two stood in a corner, talking in hushed tones. Shifter hearing was keen, so she knew they weren't talking about her. The last one made his way to her side. Roy Burgess had been a close friend of her father's and always championed her, except in this case.

"May I have a moment of your time, Skylar?"

She gestured to the chair on her left.

"What, Roy, what hasn't already been said?"

He winced, and Skylar knew she'd hit a nerve.

"Don't be like that, Skylar. I remember when you…"

She held up a manicured hand.

"Don't go there, Roy. I'm not that little girl anymore."

"No, you're not." His eyes filled with sadness. "You've changed." Before she could interject, he went on. "You had to. I get it." He glanced around the now empty room. "We all get it. Being Alpha and staying on top is the hardest job there is. You had to change to survive. But you need to think about the future. What if something happens to you? What if you're defeated? There will be no other Masons to lead us. We, and yes, I mean the council, simply cannot let anyone else become Alpha of Stone Ridge."

"Roy, I have sat here countless times and listened to every word you and the rest of the council have to say." Weary from never-ending challenges, she sighed, meeting his gaze. "I heard you. It doesn't change anything. I will mate when I'm ready. Until then, there is nothing you can do."

"Don't be too sure, Skylar."

She whipped around, facing him.

"Are you threatening me?" Her wolf growled low. She'd been quiet throughout the meeting but was sitting up and paying attention now.

"Not me," Roy said firmly. "But the others are searching for a way to force you into a mating."

"And I suppose they have a mate standing by?"

"Davis Kincaid."

Skylar's blood ran cold, her body stiffening.

"I will not, under any circumstances, mate with that man," Skylar spat out.

"He's Alpha of a prominent pack. It would be a powerful alliance."

"He's a blood-thirsty, underhanded narcissist," Skylar countered.

"I'm giving you fair warning. The others will have my head if they find out I told you." He patted her hand subtly. "Find someone suitable before they force your hand." Roy stood.

"How much time before they throw Kincaid at me?" Her voice was a whisper.

"Next full moon."

She swiveled her chair to gaze out the large window. Skylar heard Roy slip from the chamber, quietly closing the door behind him. Autumn was setting in, brilliant colors painting the trees. This was her favorite time of year. She loved running through the forest in the cool of the night. Now, more than the seasons were changing.

She had two weeks.

Skylar pulled the thick volume from the shelf, perusing the fragile pages. With a sigh, she slammed it shut, shoving it back where she got it.

"Careful, Skylar, those tomes are quite old, many irreplaceable," Anthony admonished.

She gave him a sidelong glance. Anthony Marks was one of the few who could freely speak his mind around Skylar without repercussions.

"There has to be something, somewhere, in all these books," Skylar exclaimed, frustration and aggravation rolling off her in waves. Circling, her brows furrowed as she stared at the unending expanse of ceiling-to-floor shelves filled with books. "What good does all this knowledge do if you can't find what you need?"

Anthony hid his smile behind a hand, but the crinkling laugh lines around his eyes gave it away. "Many have tried to catalog the books in this room. It's never been finished," he reminded her.

"Why not?" Skylar stared at him over the edge of a book. "I should know about this, right?"

"I thought you were aware." Anthony looked over his shoulder. "The job is apparently too intimidating, even for an Immortal. We haven't found the right person yet."

"Well, put out another ad or something. This really needs a system."

Each species of Immortals had its own laws to police their kind. Though they were all Immortal, the similarities stopped there. For instance, elves were a peace-loving breed, whereas vampires and demons thrived on blood and violence. One set of laws for all was impossible. Councils were formed, devising laws to conform to each species, ruling over their day-to-day lives.

The High Tribunal ruled over all supernatural beings. The Tribunal comprised five Immortals, each representing the larger groups of Immortals—shifters, vampires, dragons, elven, and witches. Only the most heinous acts were seen by them.

By the same token, each group's historians recorded their personal lore—lineage, battles, and noteworthy events.

The Stone Ridge wolves were one of two designated Keepers who protected the lore and laws of all Immortals. Since the beginning of recorded time, the contents had been divided evenly between shifters and vampires. The Lunar Goddess protected her moon-transitioning children—shifters, dragons, elves, gargoyles, and mermaids. Stone Ridge kept the safeguarded knowledge in the manor's library.

Whereas Lilith watched over her demon prodigy— vampires, witches, kitsune, demons, and fae.

The Eclipse library was safeguarded by the ancient vampire, Musette, in Paris, France. It was said the library was deep underground in a maze of catacombs few had ever seen.

A law stood firmly in place that any Immortal was to be granted access to the two libraries as long as an appointment was made with the Keeper. Skylar had adhered to the law through the years, like others before her.

Musette, however, tended to toy with others, be it her food, adversaries, or anyone seeking favor or admittance. Permission would be granted, but the word in the wind was whatever knowledge you were seeking was often not worth the trial of dealing with the Eclipse's Keeper.

There was something else Stone Ridge had the Eclipse did not. Thousands upon thousands upon thousands of years ago, two of the largest thefts few knew about had affected the whole of the magical world. Witches and fae had their own libraries, compiled of grimoires and spell books. Over millennia, these writings grew to be quite vast, though no one can say who was responsible. Only a few knew the location of those magical tomes. Magic undoubtedly was used. There was no other way the libraries could have been emptied instantaneously, and no one ever knew where all the magical spells were transported to.

Today, the wolf shifters of Stone Ridge lay claim to a vault. Not any vault, but *the* Vault, held tomes of magic and grimoires, the stolen collections from millennia-old witches and fae. Present-day wolf shifters couldn't tell you who stole the magical records or how it had been done. None of it had been recorded or spoken of again. The records were protected, passed down from generation to generation.

It was impossible to break into the Vault—not only was the most advanced technology used, it was also magically protected. Only a designated few had access.

"Let's not even discuss the ones in the Vault," she muttered.

"Luckily, you're searching for a loophole, not a spell," Anthony teased.

Skylar stretched her back as she gazed at the books in the vast library. There had to be a way to find what she needed. She headed toward a particular section, then searched the shelves, slowly going over the titles, pulling out the ones with blank spines.

"This entire section is wolf shifter laws and lore," she said, more to herself than Anthony, who was perusing another shelf. "There has to be something about Alphas and mates."

"Your problem is unique, Skylar," Anthony reminded her. "You're the only female Alpha. There are probably no laws regarding your situation."

Leaning against the shelf, she asked, "Then how can the council decide on my future? Shouldn't I be the one to decide when, and if, I want a mate?"

"We've been over this. It's not the mate part," he reminded her. "They're concerned about continuing the Mason line. After you, there are no more. If your brother..."

Skylar threw back her head, moonlight-pale spiral curls flowing over her shoulders, as she pinched the bridge of her nose. She felt a headache coming on, and shifters didn't get headaches.

"I know, I know... if my brother was here, he would be Alpha." She scowled at Anthony. "But he's not here. Liam's dead, just like my father and my mother before him. I've had to win countless challenges to become Alpha and stay there. I've had to be as cunning and ruthless as my enemies to prove myself... every single day for the last sixty years. I *am* Alpha of Stone Ridge, and *no one* will dictate to me when I take a mate or have a pup."

Skylar swallowed around a lump in her throat, remembering a conversation with her father. Times like this, she missed him so much, if only to talk to him for a little while.

"Dad, I don't get it. You'll always be Alpha, and you have Liam to follow you."

"Skylar, I pray you don't ever have to get it. It might not work out like that. You have to be prepared, regardless."

"I'm already going to the best schools in the country. I'm learning the business from the ground up, just like you want. I know the pack laws. What more do I need to know?"

The look he'd given her had scared her. He'd pulled her into his strong arms and hugged her tight.

"Baby girl, you'll need to know how to win. Which will be the hardest thing you'll ever do. Because it will never end. They'll keep coming for you, over and over and over."

Skylar's chest heaved from her rant. She bowed her head, immediately contrite.

"I'm so sorry, Anthony. It was uncalled for, and you didn't deserve it."

"My dear, I hardly took it personally." Her closest friend and advisor placed a calming hand on her shoulder.

"You've been keeping your emotions under a tight rein for much too long. You needed to let some of it out. I'm always here for you; you should know that."

"I have no idea what I'd do without you." She gave him a grateful smile, then let out an exasperated sigh as she stared at the multitude of books. "I still don't know what I'm going to do about the council."

"Why don't you take a break? Take a drive, go shopping... just get away from here for a little while." Anthony patted her shoulder consolingly.

"You know, that sounds like a great idea. I think I'll do just that. I'll be back later. A complicated coffee with whip cream sounds wonderful."

"Don't rush back. I'll handle everything on this end," Anthony chuckled.

"You, my friend, are worth your weight in gold... and then some."

She blew him a kiss, then made her way through the immense manor. Grabbing her keys from the sideboard, she stared at her reflection in the mirror. Other than lip gloss, she wore no makeup. She wasn't dressed to impress—comfortable, faded jeans and a soft, flowing tunic matched her mood.

Skylar needed this—a drive to no destination to rest her chaotic mind for a while.

Minutes later, Skylar was flying down the road, radio blaring. The silver Chevy Camaro was one of the few things Skylar truly enjoyed. The council would have preferred if she had a driver and a sedan, but that wasn't her and never would be. She liked driving, shifting gears, feeling the power of the car hug the curves, and flying down straight-aways. Skylar reveled in the sense of freedom.

As Alpha, she'd given up any pretense of freedom in her personal life. Every waking moment was focused on the pack, taking care of business, and solving problems. After all this time, she seldom allowed herself to think of the what-ifs. It was foolish thinking and a waste of time.

Skylar downshifted as she approached town. Easing down to a respectable speed, she made her way to her favorite coffee house. She'd use the drive-thru, then head back out on the highway.

She didn't want to take the chance of running into anyone. More often than not, it would be someone with a complaint or a problem, thinking only she could fix it for them. She took her position seriously, always giving one-hundred ten percent, but didn't she deserve a day off once in a while?

Pulling up to the menu board and speaker, she gave her order.

"Drive around, Ms. Mason. I'll have it ready in a flash."

Skylar smiled at the exuberant young voice over the speaker. She and her car were known around town. Ninety percent of Mason Falls' population were Immortals of some sort. The other ten percent consisted of humans who were fully aware of the town's supernatural element. While Mason Falls did have a mayor, he answered to the Alpha. It was her town, even though she didn't feel in charge at the moment.

As she eased up to the window, the teen was waiting for her, drink in hand. Sally Martin's kid. A single mother, she'd done an outstanding job of raising Joey. He was an exemplary student and hard-working kid, pitching in to help his mother at the local florist shop when he wasn't working at the coffee shop.

"Hey, Joey. How's it going?" Skylar handed over a twenty. "Keep the change."

"It's all good, Ms. Mason." His eyes widened at the generous tip, though her tips were well known in town. "Thanks, appreciate it."

Taking her coffee and carefully setting it in the holder, she waved to the young barista.

"See you later, say hello to your mom for me."

The open highway beckoned, and Skylar responded. For now, she was free.

About the Author

Madison Granger is a free-spirited late bloomer. She stubbornly lives by three beliefs: dreams can come true, never give up, and you're never too old to try new things. She is living proof of all three adages, vowing she isn't done by a long shot.

Born and raised near New Orleans and even closer to the swamps of south Louisiana, Madison Granger is no stranger to tales of the magical and different.

Madison loves to read, listen to music (mostly country, with a little alternative thrown in), thrives on coffee, and has had a life-long love of horses. She collects dragons, gargoyles, and angels... and anything else that catches her fancy.

Madison's stories are touched by magic and revolve around sexy Alphas, curvy, strong-willed heroines, and always a Happy Ever After.

Madison welcomes stalkers... well, the book kind anyway, and would love for you to join her journey.

Website
https://www.MadisonGranger.com/
Facebook
https://www.facebook.com/MadisonGrangerAuthor/
Readers Group
https://www.facebook.com/groups/2886808738200587
Instagram
https://www.instagram.com/madisongrangerauthor/
TikTok
https://www.tiktok.com/@madisongrangerauthor
MeWe
https://mewe.com/myworld

Milton Keynes UK
Ingram Content Group UK Ltd.
UKHW020643070923
428220UK00012B/386